Digging Up the Dead
A Tosca Trevant Mystery

by

Jill Amadio

Mainly Murder Press, LLC
PO Box 290586
Wethersfield, CT 06129-0586
www.mainlymurderpress.com

Mainly Murder Press

Editor: Judith K. Ivie
Cover Designer: Karen A. Phillips

All rights reserved

Names, characters and incidents depicted in this book are products of the author's imagination or are used fictitiously. Any resemblance to actual events, organizations, or persons, living or dead, is entirely coincidental and beyond the intent of the author or the publisher.

No part of this book may be reproduced or transmitted in any form or by any means, electronic or mechanical, including photocopying, recording, or by any information storage and retrieval system, without permission in writing from the publisher.

Copyright 2016 by Jill Amadio

Paperback ISBN 978-0-9861780-5-4
Ebook ISBN 978-0-9861780-6-1

Published in the United States of America by

Mainly Murder Press, LLC
PO Box 290586
Wethersfield, CT 06129-0586
www.MainlyMurderPress.com

*Dedicated to my tolerant and unbelievably
supportive children,
Christopher, Janet and Kathy*

*Also in the Tosca Trevant series
by Jill Amadio:*

Digging Too Deep

Digging Up the Dead 1

One

"An exhumation! You saw Raymond Chandler's dead body dug up and didn't invite me along? That is inexcusable!"

Tosca Trevant snapped open her parasol inches away from Arlene Mindel's nose, turned on her heel and marched off along Isabel Island's seafront bathed in the Southern California sun.

"*Re'm fay!*" she muttered, the Cornish curse rolling off her tongue. "Imagine going to an event as exhilarating as an exhumation and not letting me in on it. A feature story on digging up the coffin of the crime-writing legend, the creator of the cynical, fictional detective, Philip Marlowe, would be a deliciously macabre piece, although I can't possibly imagine why they did it. He died of natural causes. Still, if it turns out he was murdered, what a story! It would definitely help to promote me to crime reporter and get me back to England."

"Tosca, wait! That wasn't what happened." Arlene hurried after her friend and neighbor as fast as her chunky figure allowed.

Ignoring Arlene's shout, Tosca quickened her pace, paying no heed to the sparkling Pacific Ocean and immense Newport Beach harbor where tourists thronged Isabel Island, one of seven small islands within its bay. She still bristled at having been forced out of England five months earlier, but she had to admit that visiting with her race-car driver daughter, J.J., who now lived and competed in America, was a blessing.

Yet Tosca was still homesick for St. Ives, her hometown in Cornwall, and for her job in London. I'd fly back there tomorrow, she thought, if the royals would drop the threat of their silly lawsuit against me and my newspaper. So what if I discovered a scandal at Buckingham Palace? It wasn't their first and won't be their last.

"Tosca, wait up!"

Ignoring Arlene's shout, Tosca tightened her grip on the pink parasol and thought how nice it would be to hold a real umbrella over her head, if only it would rain, and how wonderful to have need of her wellies. She remembered for an instant she'd told J.J. she had given the rain boots away, but instead she'd secretly hidden them in her empty suitcase, now stored in a closet, hoping against hope she'd need them.

Only twice since her arrival from London had rain clouds appeared over Isabel Island. The clouds hovered barely long enough to moisten the streets before moving toward the distant San Gabriel Mountains. What I'd give for a jolly good drenching, Tosca thought, as Arlene, dressed in too-tight jeans and an oversized T-shirt, jogged as fast as she could to catch up with her.

Panting between puffs of breath, Arlene managed to say, "It was a re-burial, that's all. In his will Chandler said he wanted his wife, Cissy, to be buried with him. She died before him, and her body was cremated, but her ashes were lost until recently. After they were found in a mausoleum storage shed, Chandler's historian, Loren Latker, asked Alyssa Wayne, John Wayne's lawyer daughter, to get legal clearance so Loren could arrange a ceremony for the couple to be reunited. She did, and he did, and now Raymond and Cissy are finally together in the same grave. Isn't that romantic?"

"The same grave! I'm sorry for biting your head off, Arlene," said Tosca, slowing to a stroll and turning eagerly to her friend, "but he died more than forty years ago. I would love to have seen how he looked. Was there much decay?

Digging Up the Dead 3

Was his skeleton all in one piece? What was he wearing? Had his hair grown? That happens, you know, after you die."

"No, no. You've got it all wrong again. Good heavens, you are so bloodthirsty. The coffin itself wasn't opened, only the grave was uncovered. Cissy's ashes were in a brass urn, which was placed at Chandler's feet. Then the grave was covered up again, and a service was held."

Tosca stopped abruptly again and faced her friend.

"Did you just say, at his feet?"

"Well, yes. Cissy's urn was set at the end of the coffin where the feet are. It's customary."

"Disgraceful! You see what women have to endure? At his feet indeed. Anyway, go on and tell me the rest."

"It was a charming, nostalgic ceremony," said Arlene, "complete with a minister, hymns and a Dixieland band playing Chandler's favorite tunes. Afterwards we all went to the Whaling Bar, Chandler's old hang-out at the Valencia Hotel in La Jolla, and drank gimlets, his favorite cocktail, if you remember. Such a shame the bar has been renamed, though."

"Of course I remember the gimlets," said Tosca. "He first tasted one in England when he lived there. London's Savoy Hotel originated it with half gin, half Rose's Lime Juice, but Chandler preferred his with vodka instead. Lime juice prevents scurvy, you know."

"Scurvy? Is that some kind of scalp problem?"

"No, silly." Tosca laughed. "Scurvy was mostly a sailors' disease caused by a lack of Vitamin C. It's said that nineteenth century British admirals provided their men with lime juice during long sea voyages when there were no citrus fruits to be had."

Arlene cocked her head to consider the information. She nodded once and said, "I know that Raymond Chandler was famous for talking about gimlets, and he mentions them in *The Long Goodbye*. We drank lots of them after the reburial."

"Ah, yes, the exhumation that wasn't. All right, Arlene. I apologize, but you do see my point, don't you? Reminds me of the exhumations of other famous people. When I came to America this year I read that Christopher Columbus's body had been shunted to six burial places in three different countries before it was finally put to rest in Spain." Before Arlene could respond Tosca continued, "Indeed. And Eva Peron's body traveled here, there and everywhere. At one time Juan Peron had her disinterred and then buried in Madrid before his third wife sent Eva's body back to Argentina."

"That's bizarre. How do you know all this?"

"Don't you watch the BBC News on television? I thought everyone did. Or should. You really must broaden your horizons, Arlene. In 2012 the BBC News did an exhaustive report on famous exhumations. It was fascinating. But right now I'm focused on Chandler and Cissy."

Perhaps the re-burial, Tosca told Arlene, would provide a brand new angle for a newspaper feature about America's creator of the hard-boiled detective story.

"I could focus on Chandler's sensitivity and great love for a woman eighteen years his senior, whom he adored until his death, and how grievous it was that he had to wait more than fifty years after he died to be with her," she said. "Plus, I can make it relevant to British readers by linking it to another great passion, the Duke of Windsor's scandalous love for Wallis Simpson. She, too, was older than he. Yes, that should work."

Satisfied with her strategy but unwilling to let her friend completely off the hook, Tosca added, "You know how hard I'm trying to convince my editor to promote me. I absolutely cannot go back home and keep writing that "Tiara Tittle-Tattle" column about the royal family any longer."

"Not even with those two darling little babies that Kate and Wills have?"

"No, I've had enough of the palace and its goings-on. I am determined to be a crime reporter. This digging up of Chandler's coffin could help. He's been one of my idols for years, next to his great literary rival, Fuller Sanderson, of course. As for the gimlets, I much prefer Fuller's White Russian cocktail. Not that anything's better than my own mead, as you well know."

Arlene again cocked her head as if considering a momentous decision. "Yes, I have to say that both are favorites of mine. The writers, I mean," she added quickly at Tosca's raised eyebrows. "That Cornish wine you make is, uh, quite interesting. I'm saving the bottle you gave me for a special occasion. But I'm not familiar with the rivalry between Chandler and Sanderson. What was it about? I suppose it was because they both wrote hard-boiled mysteries."

"Yes, that, and the fact that they both fictionalized real Hollywood murder cases in their novels. For instance, in Chandler's *The High Window* he wrote about an unsolved 1929 murder and suicide at Greystone Mansion in Beverly Hills. The police at the time never figured out which of two men was the murderer. The theory is that Ned Doheny was shot by Hugh Plunkett, who then turned the gun on himself, but it's not clear-cut and hasn't been solved. Hmm. That's an idea. I might have a go at it as a cold case myself, as a matter of fact."

Two

Arlene, still panting to keep up as Tosca resumed her long-legged stride, said, "Oh, yes. I remember the Greystone Mansion case. In fact, it's a chapter in a book I bought last month called *Beverly Hills Confidential.* The detective who wrote it chronicled the notorious scandals, murders and corruption there going back to the 1920s. Did Sanderson write about the same case?"

"No," said Tosca, sitting again on the sea wall. She went on to explain that Sanderson dredged up the equally unsolved 1928 Hollywood murder of a billionaire at his home, Winchester Hall, which was fictionalized in his book, *The Total Surrender,* published around the same time as Chandler's *The High Window.*

"But I don't remember reading anything about a murder at Winchester Hall. Was it a true story?" Arlene asked, sitting down next to Tosca.

"Absolutely true. It centered on Winston Battleby's mistress shooting him five times," said Tosca. "Sanderson had his fictional detective, Johnny DiLeo, mention it, but it wasn't the focus of the book. I wonder if I should tackle solving both of those cases even if they are so old." Tosca could almost see the cogs turning in Arlene's brain. "You do know who DiLeo is, don't you? He didn't have a nickname like Philip Marlowe, who was often called Shamus—such a strange name for a private eye, but the DiLeo character was just as famous back then."

Digging Up the Dead 7

Arlene admitted that she did know a little about Sanderson, but she'd only read his first novel and half of the second one.

"His books are too gory and filled with swear words. I had to stop reading," she said, leaning toward Tosca, her words almost drowned out by a speedboat rushing by.

"Stop reading?" said Tosca. "A little too bloody, perhaps, but cursing in those days was so mild compared with today's dreadful obscenities. You don't find my Cornish swear words objectionable, do you, Arlene?"

"How could I, when I haven't the slightest idea what they mean?"

"You have a point. But let me assure you, mine are completely innocuous compared to some I could use, like *kyj dhe ves,* which I won't translate. The naughtiest thing I ever say is *kawgh ki.*" Tosca gave the phrase its harshest pronunciation.

"What does that mean?"

"Dog droppings. Another really descriptive curse I totally love translates to, 'May the devil eat your organs,' but I save that for very rude people. Anyway, Chandler and Sanderson became huge rivals. I'm surprised you don't know that. You can imagine the competition between them at book signings and author events they did together back in the 1940s and '50s. Must have been galling for Chandler since Sanderson was much younger and began publishing when he was twenty-nine. Chandler was fifty-one before his first book went on sale."

"Did one of them win out over the other at the end?"

"Chandler was and still is the champion, but others, like Dashiell Hammett and Cornwell Woolrich, came close. All were said to have left unfinished manuscripts when they died. Chandler had completed only a few chapters of *The Poodle*

Springs Story, so Robert B. Parker, who wrote the Spenser series, was asked to complete the book in the Chandler style."

"How do you know so much about our American writers?" said Arlene. She had recovered her breath and began to fan herself with a brochure she took from her purse. She nodded a greeting to a jogger who passed by.

Tosca explained that she had written several articles about American writers because she admired their style, and she enjoyed telling proper Brits about Sanderson's unconventional preference for wearing tattered shirts and going barefoot in public.

"Yes, yes," said Arlene, "but what about Sanderson's lost manuscript?"

"Ah. I heard that he left at least one, maybe more. If they exist, they are yet to be discovered. Perhaps I'll take that mystery on, too. I don't always have to investigate murders, you know. A missing manuscript is always a good story, although Sanderson's last books weren't critically acclaimed. Reviewers didn't care for them that much."

Arlene tapped Tosca's arm. "I bet you don't know that his granddaughter, Karma Sanderson, lives two streets over."

"What? Here on Isabel Island?" Tosca had started to get up from the sea wall but sat down again abruptly, her mouth wide in astonishment.

"Yes. His literary agent, Graydon Blair, does, too, and he keeps a boat here."

Tosca noted the triumphant smile, the gleam in her neighbor's eyes, and knew there was more to come. The two had become firm friends after discovering a mutual passion for gossip. Tosca came by hers naturally as the star Page Eight gossip columnist at the *London Daily Post* before her sudden reassignment to America. Arlene, an Isabel Island first-generation resident, enjoyed her own reputation as the local busybody.

Barely a week after arriving on Isabel Island, Tosca had stumbled upon some skeletal remains and hoped that by solving the mystery she could return to England in triumph, the royal lawsuit be damned. Arlene had unknowingly provided valuable information about the killer who lived nearby and whom Tosca 'unearthed,' as she liked to describe it. Although her story about catching the murderer ran in her London newspaper, Tosca wasn't able to convince her editor to give her a shot at crime reporting full-time, and she was still obliged to send in a gossip column from her new home.

"All right, Arlene. I see you are bursting to tell me something."

Three

"I heard Karma and Sally Hirsch, who is still the publisher of Sanderson's books, and Oliver Swenson, the in-house book editor, having a real heated argument," said Arlene. "Graydon Blair was there, too. I'm sure you know he took over as Sanderson's literary agent after Taylor Blair, his dad, passed away."

"Yes, I know. Where did you hear them arguing? What about?"

"The four of them were having lunch near our table yesterday at that French restaurant you like."

Tosca nodded thoughtfully. "I know Sanderson's estate kept the son on. He doesn't have the same silly nickname as his father, surely?"

"No. Graydon is too pompous to be called Tinky, although, as his family were local tailors in their day, everyone thinks it's a perfect fit. Tinker, tailor, soldier, spy."

She laughed. Tosca sensed her neighbor was about to confide more gossip, and she leaned forward expectantly, asking Arlene if the argument she heard was about book sales. She knew there was still a market among collectors for first editions of the 1940s classics.

"I don't know anything about sales or first editions," said Arlene, "but books were definitely at the center of what the shouting was all about. I heard words like 'royalties' and 'cheat.' Karma kept flapping those freckled arms of hers around, and Sally got really red in the face. It was quite a show. One word they kept repeating was 'ghost.' Did Sanderson write any paranormal books?"

"No, never, but you've told me excellent news. Definitely material for my newspaper column. Tell me more about this granddaughter," she said. "Who on earth would name a child Karma?"

Arlene explained that Fuller Sanderson's son, Norman, had married a hippie, an artist who went by the name Destiny and whose specialty was painting different versions of the solar system onto black canvases over and over and over again.

"Destiny was kind of wacky, a real character," said Arlene. "Never sold a single painting. You could smell the pot they smoked at their parties all over the island. Night and day their house was crowded with poets, artists and all kinds of riff-raff. Poor little Karma was ignored most of the time. She'd wander around the island by herself, singing songs she learned in kindergarten. I don't know why Norman put up with a lifestyle like that for a child."

Tosca nodded and told Arlene that all she knew about him was that he tried to become as famous a novelist as his father, hoping to out-write and surpass him, but never came close to Fuller's brilliance. She added that Norman's writing was once described as "muddled mediocrity."

"Anyway," Arlene continued, "after Karma's parents died six years ago, she stayed on in their little beach cottage and started up a landscaping business in Newport Beach. She may look a mess with that hair of hers and those weird clothes, but she's a wonderfully creative gardener. Several of us have her work on our yards, although I hear she's in financial difficulties. Guess her grandfather's book sales don't amount to much these days."

"Maybe not, but e-books sell well, it seems." Tosca glanced at her watch and stood up. "Sorry, I have to go. See you later, Arlene."

She patted her friend on the shoulder and began to walk off but stopped when Arlene called out, "Oh, I forgot. Karma's having a party Saturday to celebrate the forty-third anniversary of your idol's death. Would you like to come?"

"That's a strange milestone. Why not the twenty-fifth or fiftieth?"

"I have no idea, but please come to the party and meet Karma. I know you'll like her, Tosca. She's a sweet, gentle young woman."

Four

Karma ripped out the dying marigolds from their planter tubs as if attacking a bear, and flung them onto the walkway. Turning to her right, she grabbed the stems of two drooping hollyhocks and pulled. When the roots resisted her firm tug, she took a knife from the canvas tool belt around her waist and with one quick jab cut through the stems cleanly at the soil line. She exchanged the knife for her trowel and, thrusting it impatiently into the soil, dragged out the roots.

A short, stoutly built twenty-eight-year old with wavy red hair that hung around her oval face in untidy wisps, Karma Sanderson could have passed for one of Rossetti's Pre-Raphaelite women or Titian's medieval well-endowed flame-haired models, were it not for her sour expression and down-turned mouth. Muscular shoulders and a deep bosom strained at the plaid shirt she wore, her jeans caked in dirt at the knees.

After stuffing the dead flowers into a plastic sack, Karma tied its corners and hefted it onto her shoulder. She walked over to her twelve-year-old truck, parked at the curb, dumped the load into the truck bed that was already half full and returned to the garden. She stacked the empty tubs near the gate, tucked the shovel under her arm and knocked on the front door.

"All done, Mrs. Wingold," Karma told the woman who peered out. "I've planted some more geraniums and added alyssum and a giant milkweed shrub for you."

"Giant milkweed? That's a new one to me. Was there room for it?"

"Of course." Karma's expression deepened into irritation. "That's just its name. It's really quite small and blooms most of the year, but keep away from the sap it produces. It can cause a rash or something. Might be harmful."

Karma enjoyed seeing the look of alarm on the woman's face.

"Don't worry, Mrs. Wingold, you won't be drinking it, will you? On the upside is that its tiny white and purple flowers attract Monarch butterflies. Take a look for yourself. See you next month."

Karma didn't wait for a reply. She picked up the empty tubs and placed them alongside the sacks. By lunchtime she had repeated the routine five more times, planting the same mix of plants and telling each homeowner or leaving a note on the front door that she'd taken care of their yard. With a sigh she got in her truck and drove off Isabel Island across the single bridge that connected it to the city of Newport Beach.

I don't care if all those yards look the same, she thought. Makes the streets look neat and orderly. Anyway, those rich people barely notice them on the way to the yachts berthed at their private docks. I hope they'll appreciate those milkweeds after I had them shipped in free from India. I'm glad I discovered them, not that anyone ever complains about my prices. They can well afford them.

Karma headed for the twelve acres of land on the western edge of the city that her father had passed down to her after he died. Fuller Sanderson's great-grandfather had bought the fields for one dollar an acre in the early 1800s after settlers arrived in the Native American Indian territory. His will specified his land was never to be sold nor built upon, but Karma had disobeyed the directive. She had a small rustic shed erected that served as an office for the garden center she had established five years earlier. She devoted most of the acreage to plants, but large areas were neglected and left to grow wild. Dotted around were two ramshackle potting sheds, a small greenhouse, a pergola and a tiny gazebo.

Despite her efforts, success was hard to come by as there were two well-established competitors in town. Karma had not only spent Fuller's inheritance but also had gone into debt to keep afloat, buying and importing exotic plants only she, it seemed, appreciated. She considered herself a child of nature, as her mother had been, and filled the acreage with strange shrubs, flowering bushes, oddly-shaped small trees and hanging baskets of wildflowers, all plants that were proving far less popular with customers than she'd hoped.

After pulling up to the office, she slid off the vehicle's high seat and slammed the rusty door shut. I need a new truck, too, she decided. I've just got to get some money somehow. That publisher of Grandfather's books is cheating me out of royalties, I'm damned sure of it. Sally probably owes me thousands. Well, I'll call her tonight. She'd better give me some straight answers about Fuller's sales figures and bring me a statement as well as a check when she comes to my party.

"Sam?" she called, looking around for her odd-job man. Karma saw him limping toward her, his right leg dragging more than usual in the unexpectedly cool day.

"Seven more returns," he said, a cigarette butt dangling from a corner of his mouth. "Them hangin' baskets are all dyin'. You need to fill them with real flowers, not that stuff you find for free in the desert. They look pretty at first, but they're wild, Karma. You should know by now wildflowers don't last long. They start to wilt almost as soon as you dig 'em up. I see you got rid of those giant milkweeds, though. Sure are ugly. Did you decide to toss 'em?"

"Of course not. They're in some of the Isabel Island clients' front yards, except for the two I kept for myself."

"Guess you can sell anythin' that's in full bloom. The flowers are kind of pretty. Anyway, how much longer do you think you can keep this place goin'? And if you have to close, what's gonna happen to those six cats you took in? You already owe the vet a ton of money."

Karma ignored him and went into the office. On the desk were sixteen phone message slips piled onto a spike next to a large glass-topped case of mounted butterflies that were arranged by color.

Sam followed her inside. "There's all them messages about the party. Looks like everyone's comin'," he said, his wrinkled old face breaking into a smile. "Maybe this library fundraiser will help you out after all. Good idea to tie an anniversary in at the same time, though how you came up with that year, the forty-third, is beyond me. What the heck is it the anniversary of?"

"That's how old my dad and mom were when they died. Don't scratch your head like that, Sam. Anyway, I don't need any excuse, and I certainly don't need to justify myself to you."

"Okay, okay, keep your hair on, but shouldn't it be something to do with Fuller instead of his son?"

"It's personal, and anyway, the fundraiser is for Fuller's library, so it makes sense."

"Ya know, I thought I was the only one who remembers your granddaddy. He sure was kind to me when I was a kid. Hey, I forgot to write it down, but that Arlene lady wants to know if she can bring a friend, some writer type with a weird name. Tessie, Tossa or something."

"Sam, stop gabbing and unload the truck. There are bags of brush and weeds from the island gardens to put on the compost and some empty tubs that need to be cleaned and stacked."

He turned to leave, then said, "Oh, here, I caught you a couple more Western Tiger Swallowtails. They were on that patch of thistles." He pointed to a jelly jar on top of the file cabinet. Two butterflies lay motionless on the bottom. "That black one there," he tapped the side, "that's a female. Said to be deadly. Ain't that somethin'?"

Five

After Sam left the office Karma took the phone message slips off the spike and flipped through them but didn't see the message she expected. She picked up the land-line phone and dialed.

"Graydon, have you heard from Sally? Do you know if she's coming to my party? Hope she's not still mad after that argument we had. She hasn't left me a message saying she's accepted my invitation."

"I have no idea. Oh, I was thinking of stopping by your house to drop off my theremin that Bill Weinstein will be playing before I get there. He might come by tomorrow or Friday to check it out."

"I'm going home now," said Karma, "so you can come over and leave it with me."

She went out to the truck and thanked Sam for unloading the tubs, telling him to lock up when he left. As she drove off she noticed her hands on the steering wheel were covered in red blotches. Annoyed that she hadn't taken more care with the milkweeds, and figuring she'd nicked one while planting it, she hoped her hands would be clear by the time the party rolled around.

Blair was waiting at her gate with a small folding card table and the theremin. Invented by a Russian physicist researching proximity sensors, the electronic musical instrument consisted of a small black box the size of a DVR tuner that people usually hooked up to a television set. It was equipped with two metal antennas whose ether wave frequencies were programmed to catch hand movements made near them to control pitch and volume, producing eerie musical sounds often heard in sci-fi movies.

Karma led the way into her cottage and Blair set up the table and placed the theremin on it, telling Karma to move it to wherever she'd be locating the group and their instruments for the party.

"Wait a minute. What's wrong with your hands?" he said. "You'll be able to play Saturday night, won't you?"

"Of course, don't worry. I was dumb enough to get plant sap on my hands when I was working on my customers' yards. I nicked one or two of the stems by mistake and all this milky white sap oozed out. I read that it's poisonous if you drink it, imagine that, but I know better than to let it anywhere near my mouth. My hands should be okay by party time."

"All right. Let's get down to business. Where's the flash drive?" Blair's frown deepened.

"Sally has it."

"You were supposed to ask her for an extra one."

"I've been too busy," said Karma. "Don't worry, we'll get a copy."

"Damn. We need to get it from her. I'm not sure I trust the woman, her being so broke. She claims the flash drive was all she got from Oliver. He refused to give her a print-out or email her the document file. Right now she has the only copy of the file, and we need it."

"No problem. I'll call and remind her to bring it Saturday. Everything will be on the drive, right?"

"It better be."

Six

"J.J., what should I wear? A dress, jeans, shorts? Arlene told me that Karma wears hippie clothes. My leather skirt? Maybe I'll wear a cloche hat. That would be just right for Fuller's 1920s era, no?"

Tosca paused on the second step of the spiral staircase and faced her daughter. J.J. looked up from the NASCAR team racing helmet she was cleaning at the sink.

"I've never met or seen Karma, so I don't know, Mother. Some of those Newport Beach ladies like to dress up. Don't wear a hat, and definitely not that tiny skirt or hot pants you claim are shorts. I'd suggest a sundress."

"Perfect. Thank you, *keresik.*"

Tosca climbed the rest of the stairs that led to the attic of her daughter's loft-like apartment in the duplex. Designed with an open-concept plan, its one large room downstairs had space for a compact kitchen and living and dining areas. Two bedrooms upstairs book-ended a bathroom. A small landing and a French door led to the roof deck with a view of the large harbor.

Tosca took a shower and spent the better part of an hour drying and styling her waist-length, dark hair. Careful not to break into any of the operatic arias she so loved to sing but didn't to avoid disturbing their island neighbors, whose houses barely had twelve inches between their walls, she came downstairs in a pink halter sundress. She carried a pair of red high-heeled shoes. Tucked under her arm was a red and white parasol.

"Very nice," said J.J. "Wait. Is that a new parasol? What happened to the old one?"

"The handle came off. Parasols with handles are almost impossible to find. I had to settle for this."

"Mother, you're not going to need it. Please leave it here. It'll look silly because the sun's almost down."

Tosca shrugged, propped the parasol next to the front door and muttered, *"Bram an gath."*

"Mother! I'm shocked."

"Now don't get your knickers in a twist. You're giving the cuss phrase its worst meaning instead of the one I prefer, which is 'fiddlesticks'."

J.J. changed the subject. "It was very nice of Karma to invite you. Did she say you could bring Thatch along?"

"The invitation came through Arlene, and I'm sure I could have brought him if he weren't off at some godforsaken fishing hole in somewhere called Idaho. He said he was going to a nearby volcano after that, so we won't see him for at least another week."

Amateur geologist Thatcher MacAulay was a retired U.S. Secret Service agent who'd met Tosca when she first arrived on Isabel Island. The two shared an interest in mysteries, Thatch as an amateur geologist who enjoyed seeking out clues to the past through his hobby, while Tosca's natural curiosity had led her to discover and solve two crimes several months earlier.

The couple also shared a mutual, if opposite, attraction. Thatch's background trained him to be necessarily reticent as a result of his service protecting American presidents, while Tosca's career was at the other extreme as a garrulous gossip columnist. Nevertheless, they managed to complement each other.

J.J. finished wiping the racing helmet, set it on the small table near the door and turned to her mother.

"Is this the fundraiser party for the Fuller Sanderson library?" she said. "A few wealthy people should be there, and certainly some of Karma's clients. I imagine she hopes they'll be donors. Maybe some of the guests will be crime writers or in the publishing industry, so you'll feel right at home."

"Not sure if my kind of reporting qualifies," said Tosca, grimacing. "Everyone here knows me as that Brit gossip columnist who's always snooping around and cussing in the Cornish language."

"Mother, if you hadn't been digging around in the professor's garden, we'd never have known he was a murderer. Everyone read about the island killings you solved. Don't be so modest." She came closer to Tosca and scrutinized her face. "Thank goodness you've left off that awful blue eye shadow. You look a lot younger without it. You could pass for, oh, maybe forty."

Tosca grinned, her blue eyes sparkling. "*Meur ras!* Thank you. I'll take that, since my fiftieth rolls around next month, as you keep reminding me. And I'll return the compliment. You look about eighteen, not twenty-eight. " She walked into the kitchen. "Where's that mead I'm bringing to the party? It's the last jug of gooseberry I made with Acacia blossom honey, but I suppose this anniversary of Fuller Sanderson's death merits it. I hope Karma will realize its significance. I read that her grandfather devoured gooseberry pie every chance he got when he visited England."

"Quite a difference between the pie and your mead," said J.J., "but do you think you should you even be taking any, considering what happened to the last lot you gave to our neighbor?"

"Not my fault that murderous excuse for a musician deliberately laced the mead with poison and died in his cell. Must have ruined the taste. Oh, gollywobbles, look at the time." Tosca picked up the heavy jug. "See you later."

Seven

Holding her high-heeled pumps, Tosca stepped carefully down the wooden staircase that led from J.J.'s Dutch door to the front gate of the house, glancing again at the windows of the ground-floor apartment as she passed. She wondered when it would be rented. J.J. had said the owners were very fussy about tenants, and so far no one had qualified.

Tosca put on her shoes and walked to Karma's cottage. Arlene had told her that the address was two blocks south and to look for a bright green bungalow with purple window frames. It was, thought Tosca as she reached it, only too easy to spot, despite being almost hidden between the two-story homes that towered over it on each side. Isabel Island was famous for its eclectic architecture styles that ranged from modest bungalows to several marble mansions totally out of place at the beach.

The main street was filled with restaurants, boutiques, ice cream parlors, cafes, a post office and the firehouse, and it ended at the seawall and Newport Harbor. Those who wanted to cross the bay to the peninsula took the old ferry, which held three cars and several dozen passengers.

Karma's front yard was strung with red and yellow Chinese lanterns, their flickering candles mere pinpoints in the darkening sky but managing to cast shadows on the miniature palm trees leading to the open front door. Tosca tried to place the guitar music she heard from inside and determined it was the final chords from Rodrigo's haunting

"Concierto de Aranjuez" composed as a tribute to his young daughter after she died.

Almost immediately Tosca heard the mournful opening chords of the Berceuse from Stravinsky's "Firebird Suite." She couldn't figure out which instruments the musicians were playing. Definitely a guitar, and not an electric one, but what on earth was that other weird sound? She hurried through the rickety garden gate to satisfy her curiosity.

Arlene had mentioned that some of the guests would be Newport Beach socialites who were underwriters for Orange County's Performing Arts Center, where a massive sculpture of a Firebird hung above the main lobby. No doubt Karma was hoping her musical nod to their choice of décor would persuade them to write similarly large checks for the Sanderson Library she planned to build.

A cool easterly wind had picked up, and only a few people stood about on the outdoor patio, holding cocktail glasses. Two men were arguing loudly while a tall, elderly blonde woman lingered nearby, her narrow face etched into an expression of displeasure. Tosca wondered if they were some of the same people that Arlene said she'd heard arguing in the restaurant.

As she approached, her heels clicking on the stone walkway, the group turned toward her, suddenly silent. Tosca nodded as she walked by them to the open front door, where she spotted Arlene waiting for her. They greeted each other with a quick, affectionate, one-armed hug.

"Where's the hostess? I've brought the mead."

Arlene took Tosca's elbow and walked her into the cottage, which was crowded with guests.

"I'm so glad you came, Tosca," said Arlene. "Karma's set up a bar, so you can leave the jug there. I'll introduce you to her when she's finished playing."

Arlene, dressed in a long black silk gown that hugged her curves too tightly, tilted her head sideways to the back of the room, where the redhead was seated on a high stool, intent on strumming her guitar. Next to her stood a thin young man waving his hands in the air over the card table on which sat a box no larger than a small radio.

"What on earth is he doing?" whispered Tosca to Arlene. "Is he a magician or a guru performing some kind of eccentric American ritual?"

Arlene giggled, setting her chipmunk cheeks quivering. "That's Bill Weinstein. He's playing Graydon Blair's theremin. I thought it was an odd instrument too when I first saw Graydon perform with it a couple of years ago. It's an electronic instrument you don't need to touch. It works on frequencies, I was told. Makes a really eerie woo-woo sci-fi movie sound, don't you think?"

Tosca quietly agreed but thought that the strange contraption, combined with Stravinsky's despondent piece of music, was an odd choice for a party. Yet it seemed to fit in perfectly with Karma's hippie home environment. The cluttered, untidy living room with a low, beamed ceiling, small shuttered windows, and drab, olive-green rug added to a general air of gloom. The dreary atmosphere was intensified by dark blue walls covered in huge, unframed black canvasses depicting yellow and orange planets and moons.

"Those were painted by Karma's mother, Destiny," said Arlene. "She was always talking about the Universe and astrology."

Beneath the paintings and along two of the walls stretched ramshackle oak bookshelves, their contents jammed together haphazardly in untidy piles. The whole room had an air of carelessness, and Tosca hoped Sanderson's first editions weren't treated so cavalierly, if Karma owned any.

Facing the front window was a dark mahogany desk on which sat a vintage Olivetti typewriter, a briar pipe resting in a black ceramic ashtray, a jar of pencils and a few copies of Sanderson's books. Next to the typewriter was an open cardboard box containing several pages of what appeared to be a typed manuscript.

Tosca reflected that the entire room was probably exactly as the author had left it many decades earlier. She took a second look at the pipe, knowing Sanderson never smoked one, and guessed that Karma had added it to copy the items on Raymond Chandler's writing desk.

The photo Tosca had seen of Chandler's desk came to mind. It showed several more items than on Sanderson's desk, including the movie script of *The Blue Dahlia,* a box of chessmen and a brass stamp holder. Had Karma set up Sanderson's desk as a deliberate parody, she wondered, or was it mere hubris? Perhaps she wanted to invoke an image of Sherlock Holmes, whose long-stemmed curved pipe was mentioned often in the Conan Doyle books.

"I don't believe we've met," said a tall, pink-haired young woman, holding out her hand. "Charlotte Carver."

Dressed in a low-cut taffeta gown that matched her hair, with layers of ruffles around the hemline, she swayed forward enough for Tosca to detect liquor on her breath. The woman over-corrected herself, leaning back.

"How do you do? I'm Tosca Trevant. Very pleased to meet you."

"Do I detect an accent?" The word came out 'assent.'

"Indeed, yes," said Tosca. "I'm from Cornwall."

"What's that? Some new state we just added on? I can't even remember the names of the twenty-seven we already have."

"Cornwall is in the United Kingdom, at the bottom, below England. I'm from St. Ives. It's on the left, if you look at a map."

Charlotte gaped and tottered off toward the bar, leaving Tosca to inspect the other guests. She looked around the room and was delighted to see that a few of the women wore calf-length, tight black skirts with slits up the sides and black stockings with seams running up the back, reminiscent of the 1940s fashions in Fuller Sanderson's books. Three of the women wore little, flat, pancake-style hats tilted to one side, recently made popular again by the Duchess of Cambridge.

Two red velvet wing armchairs, missing most of their brass nail trim, were occupied by a couple of women in gold and scarlet caftans and thick platform shoes with ankle straps. Bloomsbury fans, Tosca mused, thinking of the group of London intellectuals, artists and writers who had been famous in the early 1900s.

Eight

Sitting on the tattered peacock-blue sofa facing the chairs was an elderly man squeezed between two Downton Abbey-style dowagers, their hair fashioned into styles of the era.

Tosca's gaze swung to the worn beige cotton rug against the far wall where a group of hippies with unkempt hair and in frayed denim cutoffs and T-shirts lounged on the floor. They were whispering among themselves and breaking into occasional laughter. Friends of Karma, Tosca assumed. Off in one corner on a loveseat sat a woman who appeared fast asleep, her head on her chest, curled over like a hedgehog.

Arlene came to Tosca's side, asking what she thought of the crowd, the cottage and the party in general.

"I'm having a wonderful time," Tosca said. "The whole experience is fascinating. Who's that woman in the slinky leopard-print dress slit all the way up her thigh? The one with the young man wearing a cravat. Mother and son?"

Arlene giggled. "No, Tosca. They're a December-April item."

"Oh, you mean she's a jaguar."

"Jaguar?"

"Yes, older woman, younger man. Don't you have that expression here?"

"You must mean cougar."

"Ah, cougar, is it? At least they're all from the same cat family."

"Time for you to have a cocktail," said Arlene, taking her friend's arm. "Let's go and get a drink."

The most popular spot was an oak table that served as the bar, its surface almost completely covered by two large trays of liquor. A bottle of Tanqueray gin stood between three stately bottles of Grey Goose and the more pedestrian Absolut. Whiskey, sherry and several liqueurs, including Kalua, Chambord and Tia Maria, crowded out the cocktail, wine and lowball glasses. A bucket of ice held a carton of heavy cream wedged halfway down in the midst of the cubes. In the center of the table was a large photo of Fuller Sanderson holding a cocktail glass filled with a cream-colored liquid.

"His favorite drink, a White Russian," murmured Tosca to Arlene as they approached the bar.

"Would you like one?" asked a voice behind her.

Tosca turned to the young woman who had been playing the guitar, taking in the gypsy-style dress and the several long strands of beads that festooned her neck, among them a large crystal pendant. Tosca judged instantly that this was Karma and must favor her mother because she had none of the Sanderson side of the family's fine, almost delicate, features.

Karma's long face appeared even longer due to the dangling gold hoops that dragged at her earlobes and hazel eyes whose outer edges tilted down toward a nose that drooped unattractively. Her thick red hair, masses of it piled upon her head, was her best feature and, thought Tosca, saved her from being nondescript.

"I'm Karma," the woman said, offering her hand. "Welcome to my home. I hear you are a Johnny DiLeo fan, that you sing opera, the queen kicked you out of England, and you come from Cornwall."

"How on earth do you know all that?"

"It's a small island," said Karma.

Tosca hastened to explain that she was indeed a fan of Sanderson's fictional detective, that her singing was strictly confined to the bathtub, because although she came from a family of opera singers, she was not one herself, and yes, she was a Cornishwoman. As for Her Majesty, Tosca admitted the palace had been instrumental in her reassignment to America.

"We all know you, too," said Karma, "for finding out how Professor Whittaker's wife died. Here, let me make you a White Russian. Then I'll introduce you to the friends of mine with whom I think you'll have the most in common."

At Tosca's raised eyebrows Karma added, "They're in the publishing business."

She mixed the White Russian, handed it to Tosca and steered her toward a short, overweight blond man in his forties and an elderly, white-haired woman

"These are two of my dearest friends," Karma told Tosca, "and the most important people in Grandfather Sanderson's legacy. Meet Sally Hirsch, whose company still publishes his books, and Oliver Swenson, our editor and the writer I want to work on the manuscript or manuscripts that Fuller is said to have left. Once we find it—or them, that is. We've been searching everywhere for years."

Nine

Tosca shook hands with each in turn, taking Sally's first, her fingers as dry as twigs, then Swenson's fleshy, plump hand that felt like unkneaded dough. Sally smiled a greeting. Her thick make-up failed to cover the wrinkles her smile produced all over her plain features, but her expression was a sincere one.

In contrast, Swenson's thick lips barely moved, his chin sunk into a thick neck with two rolls of fat. His girth was mostly due to a bulging beer belly that strained at the buttons of his plaid shirt. Nevertheless, Tosca found herself fascinated by his eyes, a pair of perfectly matched black pearls glistening with bold intensity as he stared at her.

"Ah, yes. Oliver. I read in *Publishers Weekly* that you will be working on Fuller's manuscript if it shows up. Quite a challenge."

"Not really," he said, his tone disdainful. With a quick motion that Tosca judged was a practiced one, he flicked back the unruly lock of fair hair hanging over his forehead.

"I am intimately familiar with his style," he said. "I can quote much of his writing, particularly the last book published just before he died." Swenson glanced pointedly at Sally, who looked away.

Tosca sought to fill the uncomfortable silence that followed. "Hirsch House has always published Sanderson's books, I believe," she said, addressing Sally. "A wonderful treasure of works."

Digging Up the Dead

"Yes, we've been fortunate enough to handle his books ever since Fuller wrote his first novel, a brilliant debut for one so young," she said. "My father owned the company but passed away several years ago. Happily, we still enjoy a great, successful partnership with Karma and Graydon, although these days many of us in publishing are hurting due to the ebook revolution. Sanderson's books are sold on the online Amazon web site, of course, but Chandler far, far outsells him. Sales for Fuller's ninth and final novel before he died have, in fact, been disappointing."

Swenson snorted. "You should have promoted it more. You spent hardly any money on publicity or for a book tour."

"You know very well, Oliver, that Fuller was not a well man back then. He was in no condition to travel. He died only two months later."

Sally glared at the editor and gulped down her cocktail, then tipped the glass upside down toward Karma as if to say, "Look, my glass is empty." Karma broke the impasse by announcing she'd better help her guests mix up some more White Russians and went over to join them. Swenson followed but stopped when he heard his name called. He turned to the front door, where a tall man, his gray hair tied back in a short, neat queue, had entered followed by an elegant fiftyish blonde. Despite his height and muscular build the man moved like a cat, softly and surely.

"All's well, right?" he asked Swenson, slapping him on the back. Aware of Tosca's gaze, the newcomer turned to her and extended his hand. To her surprise his fingers were sweaty. They barely touched her own and were quickly withdrawn.

"Graydon Blair," he said. "I am Fuller Sanderson's agent of record and continue to be, despite his death." His pompous tone set Tosca's antennae vibrating. "And this is Cynthia Turner," he added.

The blonde, her smooth shoulder-length hair falling across one side of her face, shook hands. Tosca was impressed with the woman's old Hollywood glamour, noting the Lauren Bacall hairstyle and slinky white satin dress that clung to her body and fell in folds to the floor.

After shaking hands with Cynthia, Tosca turned back to the agent, wondering if the man always pronounced his occupation in capital letters.

"I'm Tosca Trevant," she said. "I am very familiar with your name, Mr. Blair. I'm a huge Sanderson enthusiast and a keen student of his life. I've been hearing about a lost manuscript. Is it true?"

"Perhaps more than one manuscript, dear lady, more than one, we believe. Karma was telling me last week you are a gossip columnist. Do you write anything literary that would be considered worth reading?" he said.

"Occasionally *Kernewek, penn bras*," said Tosca, smiling sweetly.

"Hmm. A foreign language. Not one I've heard before, and I'm sorry to tell you that it fails to pique my interest."

Blair stepped away, gripping Cynthia's arm as he guided her toward the bar.

"Good gracious, Tosca," said Arlene who'd been hovering nearby. "He was kind of rude. Just out of curiosity, what did you say to him?" said Arlene.

"I simply told him 'occasionally the Cornish, you fathead.' It's true. I have written several articles about the Cornish and our language."

They grinned at each other.

"For a bookish man Mr. Blair looks very fit," said Tosca.

"He is. He run marathons all the time and wins quite a few."

"Tell me about his bit of totty," said Tosca. "I'm interested in a woman who doesn't appear to mind being outshone by her partner's flamboyance."

"Totty?" said Arlene.

"Yes, you know, bit of skirt. It's English, dear, plain English." Tosca shook her head in exasperation.

"Oh. Okay. I don't know a lot about Cynthia. I do know she tells people she was once engaged to a Saudi prince, but every blonde in Newport Beach claims that. They all hang out at the Greenways Hotel's penthouse nightclub."

"She's wearing some beautiful jewelry."

"Cynthia owns a jewelry store," said Arlene, "and has a second store, a boutique, really, at the Barracuda Bay Club, which does very good business. I heard she's an expert with diamonds. Did you see her sneering expression when she saw that big old fake jewel our hostess is wearing? I'm surprised she didn't tease Karma about it. She's been known to insult people for wearing costume jewelry."

Tosca's attention swung over to Blair at Cynthia's side as he stood drinking and twirling a stubby, white enameled cigar holder. Despite its thickness, Tosca admired its elegant Art Deco 1920s design and the silver band but wondered why a plastic cap covered the opening for a cigar, and a piece of tape extended over the other end of the holder. She decided they acted as barriers to dissuade Blair from smoking. Pretty clever, she thought

"Have you ever seen him smoke cigars in that thing?" she asked Arlene.

"Can't say I have, Tosca. Excuse me, I want to catch Nora over there."

Ten

Arlene hurried off while Tosca continued to study Sanderson's agent. She decided Graydon Blair had to have come posthaste to Karma's party straight from a beauty spa. He appeared to have been massaged, groomed and polished from head to toe. His hair barely covered the bald areas that gleamed in the candlelight, and his pink skin glowed like the face of a porcelain doll. He wore three rings, but she daren't check his glossy nails closely for fear they'd blind her. Blair's pale blue silk shirt, a perfect color match to his small, suspicious eyes that darted constantly around, was tailored to his figure with tucks on each side and a single breast pocket. His starched jeans had a crease she was sure could cut through melons.

What impressed Tosca most about the man was his air of supreme satisfaction with himself, that mysterious smug aura that surrounds some people after sensational sex. Had Blair's massage, if he'd had one that day, included a quickie? Tosca smiled inwardly and mentally shook herself out of her daydream. She saw him set his glass down on the desk, still fiddling with the cigar holder. She waited to see if he'd remove the cap and tape in order to insert a smoke and light up. Instead, he continued to play with it. Then he went over to Sally and took the glass from her hand.

"Here, let me get you another." Tosca heard him say.

Blair gave Sally a quick kiss on the cheek and joined Karma where the line for refills was seven deep. An older man in a fur-trimmed brown suede vest offered his place to

Blair, but the literary agent declined. Still fascinated with him, Tosca wondered why Blair kept giving up his own place in line until everyone else had fixed themselves a drink or taken a bottle of beer. Perhaps her assessment of him as rude was misplaced. Finally, he was the last one.

"There you are," said Arlene, distracting Tosca from her scrutiny of Blair. "Have you met Nora? She just got back from safari in Kenya."

Tosca shook hands. As they exchanged pleasantries she noticed Blair hand Sally her fresh drink. Arlene and Nora began gossiping about the various guests, and Tosca listened eagerly, hoping for scandal. She'd learned hardly any since arriving on Isabel Island, except for the plight she'd found herself drawn into shortly after arriving from London.

Tosca learned that the young blonde in the striped dress was engaged to a vice president of General Electric who'd taken forty-seven years to reach his lofty title, that the old fellow in the dark blue corduroy jacket had just lost his young boyfriend to a wealthier man, and that the dark-haired hippie on the floor near the sofa was just out of jail for possession of heroin. The girl next to him was the daughter of a millionaire who lived near Karma and had been ordered into rehab for six months but had left the facility to come home. Arlene also said that Karma's outrageously large pendant was typical of the gaudy costume jewelry the young woman favored.

Tosca found none of the information salacious enough or uncommon enough to warrant a newspaper column item, and she was inclined to tell Stuart, her editor in London, that he might as well kill off the American version of her English "Tiara Tittle-Tattle" column. There was simply nothing to report in California except a crime or two she hoped would materialize.

"Fascinating," said Tosca to Arlene, "but did I hear an English accent over there?"

Arlene looked toward the side of the room Tosca indicated with her chin. "Yes, that's Emily, one of our major Newport Beach socialites. She sponsors everything, it seems—or rather, her husband does. He's co-founder of Monolith Airlines. I should introduce you. I forgot she might be here."

She and Tosca walked over to Emily, where Arlene made the introductions, explaining that Tosca had arrived from London several months earlier. The two Brits shook hands.

"How do you do?" said Emily. "Tosca Trevant? You can't be the gossip columnist who writes for that dreadful *Daily Post,* surely?"

Tosca figured that if the woman's nose was pointed any higher toward the ceiling, her neck would snap.

"Oh, yes, I certainly am that person." Tosca was beginning to enjoy herself. "I'm collecting gossip on this side of the pond, too, for that dreadful *Daily Post,* including about Brits who live here. Of course, Newport Beach does not have quite the Buckingham Palace ambience, but I find Americans are far more interesting than the expats."

"But how are you managing the culture shock? It took me absolutely ages to adapt," said Emily. "In fact, in many ways I never have, because it's so different here."

"How long have you lived in California?"

"Eighteen years." Tosca watched with amusement as the woman's lip curled in derision.

"How sad. Perhaps you should go back to the U.K. For myself, I deeply appreciate Americans. They are the most generous people in the world. Have you forgotten that in World War II they saved our arses?"

With that parting shot pronounced in her best Queen's English, Tosca turned away, catching Emily's shocked expression out of the corner of her eye.

"The next person who goes wittering on about being British and how they dislike it here, I just might strangle," she said under her breath. "Those who miss rain are excepted, of course."

In her haste to leave Emily she bumped into Blair, causing him to drop his cigar holder. He bent immediately to retrieve it, as did Tosca, and their heads met as they both rose. Tosca was the first to laugh, expecting him to do the same but his attention was on the holder he clenched in his fist.

"So sorry," she said, "I was admiring your cigar holder. I thought I'd seen it with a cap on, but I must have been mistaken. Is it a Meerschaum?"

But he'd already moved away to the bar.

"I see you've been giving Graydon Blair the once-over," said Arlene, coming to her side. "Looks like he's brought his medieval harp. Graydon is known to collect odd musical instruments."

"How successful is he as the son of Taylor Blair, Fuller's literary agent?"

"No idea, but the gossip is he's not doing well. He might have to sell his house and maybe even his boat. Graydon's the one I told you was arguing with Sally, Karma and Oliver Swenson at the restaurant the other day. He owns the theremin Bill was playing."

Before Tosca could reply, Karma's voice cut through the chatter to announce she and Bill would play one more piece, and later in the evening they would be joined by Graydon on his rare Kinnor harp.

"His lyre, she means," Tosca said quietly to Arlene.

The words were barely out of her mouth when she heard a deep voice whisper her name in her ear and found herself spun around and enveloped in a bear hug.

"Thatch!" Tosca's delight at seeing Thatcher MacAulay was written all over her face. "You've come home early. Catch any fish? Finished digging? Bring back any rocks?"

"Blizzard."

As usual, she smiled at his terse reply. She'd learned to read behind the words of the retired Secret Service agent she'd met a few months earlier. His amateur hobby as a geologist had helped Tosca solve a murder soon after she'd arrived from England, and the two had begun a cautious romance, both having lost their spouses a few years earlier and still nervous about dating again in mid-life.

"How did you know I was here? I turned my mobile off," she said, studying his six-foot, three-inch frame, suntanned, lined face, and the thick salt-and-pepper hair that earned him his nickname.

"J.J.," he said.

Tosca and Thatch had found something they shared in common: Each had a daughter in her late twenties, although Thatch's daughter, Christine, lived in a residential half-way house for schizophrenics. He also had a son, Andy, who was a bicycle cop on Isabel Island and was responsible for introducing Tosca to Thatch when she began to unravel a murder mystery at a neighbor's island home. She had almost pushed Andy off his bike to get his attention, and since then the MacAuley family and the Trevants had become friends.

Eleven

At the sound of three short peals Tosca and Thatch turned to see Karma holding up a small brass temple bell and hitting it with a tiny wooden mallet. The musicians had stopped playing, and everyone waited for Karma to speak.

"Thank you all so much for coming tonight," she said, "to celebrate my grandfather and his books. It is also to honor my parents who were both aged forty-three when they died, so that's why I call it the forty-third anniversary. I've invited you all here tonight to give me your financial support for the Fuller Sanderson Library. I hope to finalize the building plans next month with David Wicks, my architect over there." Karma waved in the direction of the red sofa and continued, "We'll soon get the permits and everything else in motion. The site has already been staked out at my garden center, the land Fuller left to my father, and which is now mine, as you know. Thank you all again. Please have another drink while Graydon gets set up for more entertainment. He's brought his little harp. Bill will continue to play Graydon's theremin."

Blair stepped to Karma's side, holding the harp still in its carrying case.

"Just one thing, if you'd be so kind," he said, addressing the crowd." I'd very much appreciate it if you would not take photos when I play. The Kinnor is very special, and I don't want any thieves knocking at my door." He smiled to soften the words and returned to the bar.

The immediate buzz of conversation and a general surge toward the liquor drowned out Tosca's comment to Thatch.

"Let me get you a drink," she repeated more loudly. "Want to try a White Russian?"

"Beer, please." He nodded toward the front door, indicating a retreat into the front yard away from the noisy crowd. Tosca nodded in understanding and went to the bar. She noticed Graydon had left his cigar holder next to the line of glasses. She picked it up, wondering if it was one of the Royal Meerschaums so popular in England for their natural filters that her grandfather had enjoyed. Noting no brand name as she turned it around, Tosca saw that it appeared to be new with no sign of use. She replaced the holder next to the glasses, where she'd found it.

Tosca went out to the patio to bring Thatch back inside, remembering she hadn't introduced him to their hostess. They re-entered the living room. Karma had retrieved her guitar and was sitting on the stool, strumming and preparing to play alongside Blair on his harp and Bill on the theremin.

Pulling Thatch by the hand, Tosca brought him over to her. "Karma, this is a friend of mine, Thatcher MacAulay."

"Welcome. I sure hope you enjoy our music," Karma said, stopping her playing long enough to shake hands and then continuing to tune up her guitar. Bill stood in front of the theremin and switched it on, arms raised. Blair rolled up the sleeves of his shirt, checking that they were of equal length on his forearms, and nodded at Karma. They began to play.

She watched Bill waving his hands above the theremin like a conductor without a baton, gazing seriously at the ceiling. Karma's large hands moved awkwardly over the guitar strings, and Blair plucked at the harp. The combination of their instruments produced, in Tosca's opinion, the worst cacophony she'd ever heard.

Tosca and Thatch looked at each other and backed away behind the crowd. They went out again into the garden and sat on the wrought iron garden chairs, listening to the strange sounds that wafted through the open door and windows.

"Tell me about the woo-woo thing that belongs to Mr. Dazzle," said Thatch.

"Sorry, I've never seen or heard of one like that before. I'm going to have to pay him a visit sometime and ask about it. I'm fascinated. Why don't you go get that twangy thing you play and join them? I'm sure they wouldn't object if you sat in. Maybe they'd stop and just listen to you."

"With my uke? Not tonight, Tosca. I'm a tad weary from driving."

After several minutes the guitar abruptly stopped playing in the middle of a tune.

"Do you think that's the end?" said Thatch. "Hope so."

They heard Karma swear loudly.

"Sounds like she's busted a string," said Thatch. "An experienced guitarist would keep going by just using a different string, but let's hope the concert is over, and I can get another beer."

He and Tosca stepped inside the living room where some of the partygoers were commiserating with Karma, who was holding her guitar. One of the strings was hanging loose. Blair announced that Bill would continue to play the theremin, and he would play his rare harp, with an emphasis on the word, 'rare.' As tepid applause in appreciation for more music died away, a piercing scream sliced the air.

Twelve

"Stand back! Give her room!"

One of the guests rushed forward. "I'm a doctor," he said. "Call 911!"

Everyone instantly pulled away, and Tosca saw Sally lying on the floor near Fuller's desk, a broken glass nearby and what looked like the remains of her White Russian cocktail spreading across the carpet. Her limbs were shaking, and her entire body began to convulse. In response to the urgent demand, almost all of the guests rushed to find their cell phones in their pockets or in the purses they'd left on chairs or in Karma's bedroom.

"I've got a dispatcher on the line already," a man yelled, and continued talking into his phone.

Arlene clutched Tosca's arm, trembling noticeably as husbands and wives sought out each other and huddled in shock. Thatch put his arm around Tosca, and Karma continued to kneel on the floor at Sally's side, trying to hold her hand as the violent shaking continued to wrack the elderly woman's body. Swenson stood next to her, gazing down in horror. Blair hurried over, his face expressionless.

"Anyone know if she has epilepsy?" asked the doctor, checking Sally's neck and wrists.

"What's he doing?" whispered Tosca to Thatch.

"He's looking to see if she is wearing an ID bracelet or pendant that would indicate she suffers from seizures."

"Poor woman," Arlene said quietly, calming down. "Probably too many of those White Russians that I saw her guzzling down like water. Hey, she didn't drink any of your mead, did she? Look what happened to Professor Whittaker when you gave him some. Sorry, couldn't resist."

"Maybe Sally should have skipped the hard liquor and had my wine instead. I hear sirens."

Karma ran outside to flag down the ambulance and a fire truck. Both pulled up outside, double-parking along the one-way street. A police cruiser joined them. Two paramedics unloaded a gurney and carried it into the bungalow along with an IV and other medical equipment. They checked Sally's vital signs, lifted her onto the stretcher and wheeled it out to the ambulance, saying she'd be taken to Sheldon Hospital.

"I'll follow in my car," Karma announced to the guests. "Please stay on, all of you, and try to enjoy the rest of the evening. I'll let you know how she is as soon as I can. No, Graydon, no need for you to come, too. I'll be fine," she said as Blair came to her side. She knelt to pick up Sally's raffia tote bag from the floor, its contents scattered under and around Fuller's desk.

"Here, she'll need this at the hospital," Arlene said, picking up a slender beige leather wallet and giving it to Karma. "They always want to see insurance cards before they even start trying to save your life these days."

After the ambulance, the fire truck, the police and their hostess left, most of the guests lingered for a while, then said their goodbyes to each other. Among those who remained there was muted talk, and several had already encircled the oak table to refill their glasses. Charmaine, an elderly woman who had been introduced to Tosca as a friend of Karma's parents, gathered up the spilled contents of Sally's bag and set them on Fuller's desk. They included a lipstick, a packet of tissues, a silver business card case, a Honda key fob with several keys on it, and a silver locket on a long, oval-link chain.

"This must be Karma's," Charmaine exclaimed, holding up the small heart-shaped pendant. "It has her grandmother's name, Abigail, engraved on it. A gift from Fuller to his wife, I guess, and passed on down to Karma."

Blair, Swenson and a few others craned their necks to see it. No one remarked on the fact that it had been in Sally's purse. Tosca figured they were too embarrassed to say anything, and it was quickly set on top of the desk along with the other articles. The largest and strangest item that had tumbled half-out of its box from Sally's bag was a lavender and rose-colored glass-like object that had landed at Tosca's feet. She picked it up, surprised at its weight because of its delicate design, and was still holding it when the ambulance left.

Shaped like a miniature candelabra, its four small tubes appeared made to hold tiny tapers. Its heaviness led Tosca to guess it was a piece of carved gemstone, but she had never seen anything as odd or so colorful. A small silver plaque on the crystal base bore the word "Sunida."

As she stood examining it and admiring its beauty, Thatch practically snatched it out of her hands, turning it around and around, repeatedly exclaiming, "Good God!"

"What? What is it?" said Tosca,

"It's the Tourmaline Chandelier," he said. "The twin to the Candelabra tourmaline from the Queen Mine in San Diego. No one knew who bought this one after it was found in the Oceanside Mine." Thatch held the tourmaline up to the light. "It's an extraordinary, extremely rare, museum-quality piece. The other one, the Candelabra, was the tourmaline find of the century. It's on display in the Smithsonian Institution.

This one is slightly smaller and disappeared shortly after it was discovered."

"It's beautifully textured. Look at the ridges. Did someone carve it?"

Thatch laughed. "No, the striations are naturally formed. It was extracted from the mine exactly as you see, polished up, of course. I wonder if it could be Sally's?"

"Sally's? But the name or word on it is 'Sunida,'" said Tosca, pointing to the plaque. "Wonder where she got it?"

"Sunida sounds like it could be a Thai name. I can't believe I'm holding the Chandelier. It's worth close to a million dollars," said Thatch, "a very expensive bauble."

He handed it to Charmaine, who put it back into the box and said, "We should leave everything here on the desk. Karma can sort it all out when she comes home."

She placed the box next to Sally's other belongings on Fuller Sanderson's old writing desk.

The heart had gone out of the evening, and the guests drifted off, walking to their island homes or heading for the ferry to return to the peninsula. Those who had driven from the mainland got into their cars to cross the bridge to Newport Beach.

"I think I'll spend the night on my boat," announced Blair. "It could be hours before we hear anything from Karma. There's a full moon. Might even do some night fishing. Oliver, like to join me?"

Swenson turned his back and lumbered out the door without replying.

Blair shrugged, grimaced and said, "Goodnight, ladies," as he, too, left.

Thirteen

Tosca looked around the living room. "The least we can do is clean this place up now that everyone's gone. Thatch, could you make sure the candles in the Chinese lanterns in the yard are out? Thanks. Arlene, perhaps you'd take the glasses and dishes to the kitchen. There's probably a tray in the kitchen you can use. I guess we'll leave all that booze on the table. I'll mop up the mess on the carpet."

"Sure, be happy to. The White Russian she was drinking has soaked in real good, looks like. Might be difficult to get the stain out."

Arlene picked up the carton of cream, went into the kitchen and placed it next to three similar cartons in the refrigerator. After half an hour the three decided they'd done the best they could to ensure that Karma came home to a semblance of order although, as Tosca confided to Arlene as they bade each other goodnight, Karma might not even notice, given the slovenly state of the house.

"I agree," said Arlene, "but her garden center is beautifully neat and organized, and she does a great job with our yards. Another thing I give her credit for is rescuing special needs cats. Oh, here, this must be yours. I found it near the window when we were cleaning the carpet." She handed Tosca a two-inch black flash drive. "Probably slipped off your keychain. I notice you always have a couple of them on there."

"Arlene, I've never seen this one before. It's not mine."

"Must belong to one of the guests, then, or to Karma. Hold on to it for now. We can check with her tomorrow. Such a sad ending to the party. Sure hope Sally's all right. Well, goodnight again."

After Arlene left Tosca felt Thatch's arm around her shoulder.

"It's only ten o'clock, Tosca. How about a drink at the tavern? Oh, are you taking the Chandelier with you?" he said.

"After you told me its value, I don't feel comfortable leaving it. I don't see any way to lock the front door. There's no deadbolt or mechanism to secure it. If this thing is not Karma's, she won't know its value and might not take good care of it, judging by the lack of security here. I'll bring it back tomorrow."

"Good plan. How about a drink?"

"After what we just went through with Sally, poor thing, I'm not in the mood. Come home with me and have a glass of mead. I have a fresh batch ready for sampling. It's almost as good as the blackcurrant they make at Ninemaidens Mead in Redruth, Cornwall. Aren't you tempted?"

By now Tosca was well aware of Thatch's aversion to her home-brewed wine, and she took every opportunity to tease him about it.

"Nine maidens?" he said. "Where do you Brits get these wild names?"

"Thank you for not calling me English now that Cornwall is officially recognized as a cultural minority like Wales, Scotland and Ireland. I'm thrilled. Now, Ninemaidens, Thatch, actually is a real place, a magical area. It's an ancient monument, a row of nine granite megaliths that legend says were a group of young girls who were turned to stone for dancing on the Sabbath. The Ninemaidens meadery itself has beehives all over Cornwall, and probably some are near the monument, though I think they are based in Truro."

"Sweetheart, I love all your tales, but right now I know you have some beer in the fridge unless J.J. and her pals have snagged it all. Let's go."

They left Karma's cottage, closing the door carefully behind them, and walked the few blocks to Tosca's house.

"Wonder what's on this flash drive," she said, taking it from her bag. "I suppose it must be Karma's, but perhaps it fell from Sally's purse."

"Oh, no, you're not about to start nosing around again, are you?" said Thatch. "Nearly got you killed the last time you got curious."

"I'll just take a quick peek, I promise, *keresik*."

"Man, when you call me that I go all a-tingle," Thatch laughed, "or I would if I remembered what it meant."

"What? You've forgotten already? You know very well it's a term of endearment."

"Hmm. Before I leave tonight I will return the nice sentiment." He tried to pronounce the word only to set Tosca laughing.

"Oh, dear, love, you've still got it wrong. The man says *keresigyon*, to a woman, not *keresik*."

"Yeah? I think I'll stick to good ol' 'sweetheart' from now on. So are we on for a drink?"

"Oh, one more thing, Thatch. What about the pink sculpture that fell out of Sally's purse? I'd like to know who the person called Sunida is, the name that's engraved on it."

"I doubt if it's much of a mystery, and besides, it's none of your business, although that's never stopped you before." He smiled to soften his criticism, then added, "As I told you, Tosca, it's an extremely valuable piece. You know, I wouldn't mind knowing who owns it myself." Thatch opened the small wrought iron gate at Tosca's house.

"But don't you think it's strange that Sally had two other women's belongings in her purse? We know who Abigail is, and Sally, of course, but who is Sunida, a man or a woman? I asked Arlene, who knows everything that goes on here, and she said she had no idea. You know I can't resist a puzzle, especially if it concerns Fuller. Let's find out."

"Tosca, I admit I am intrigued by the Chandelier and its disappearance for three decades, but who says it's connected to Fuller?"

"Oh, don't be such a wet blanket."

Fourteen

"What's that awful smell?" said J.J., sniffing loudly as she came through the front door and set her backpack down. The race helmet tied to one of its buckles bounced as it hit the floor.

"Ah, hello, love. How was your day?" said Tosca. "I assume you stayed overnight in Long Beach? How about an early lunch?"

"Not if what you're cooking smells like that, Mother. It's vile."

"Pungent, perhaps, I'll concede that. I'm making metheglin from an old Welsh recipe. It has a marvelous bouquet and flavor. A change from regular mead, although it's similar. This one calls for rather strong herbs. I doubt it will be as good as Cornish metheglin, but I am giving it a try."

Tosca added a lid to the small pot she'd been stirring. She rinsed the wooden spoon in the sink, placed it on a plate next to the stove, and took a seat on one of the two high stools at the kitchen counter.

"Whatever it is, it stinks," said J.J.

"But I use only the very best natural ingredients in my mead. Unfortunately, I am now living in a country whose honey bees, I suspect, do not work as hard as ours in Cornwall, and when they do decide to collect nectar, the plants are probably genetically altered. However," she said with a sigh, "I carry on. That's what we Brits must do in times of strife."

J.J. guffawed. "Come off it, Mother. Stop dramatizing. Anyway, you haven't told me what's in the pot."

"Alas, I've had to compromise to make this next batch of wine. I bought some Turkish honey."

"What?"

"Yes, made in Turkey. Their bees forage their nectar from Turkish Pines, among other plants. Says it right on the label. I'm boiling the honey to reduce it down, but it can't be the honey that smells. I was going to use Albanian honey, but it lacks character. For this batch I'm not sure what the result will be, but I figure it's worth a try. I added some herbs, too, maybe that's the problem. Does it really stink?"

J.J. rolled her eyes as she went to each window to open it, and pulled the door back to its hinges. "Which herbs?"

"Umm, I am not exactly sure. I found them at the Asian market that Arlene told me about. I told the Chinese lady that I was making metheglin and needed something to give it strength. So she sold me these." Tosca held up a large plastic bag of dried yellow leaves and dark brown pellets that looked like bark. "Do you think she misunderstood? She spoke barely any English but was very enthusiastic about these."

Grabbing the pot off the stove and snatching the plastic bag from Tosca, J.J. ran down the steps to the alley behind the house, and threw both items into the garbage can as Tosca watched helplessly from the back window.

"You owe me one pot," J.J. told her mother when she came back upstairs.

"That was a bit drastic, don't you think? You know, love, if there were some meadows nearby I could have collected my own elderflowers along with balm and mace. but all I see outside is hundreds of boats and unending sunshine."

"Don't go off again about your need for rain, Mother. Talking of which, I gotta go take a shower."

J.J. ran up the spiral stairs to the bathroom.

Tosca stood in the kitchen. unsure what to do about the turn of events. She had planned to spend the whole day making the spicy mead and setting it to mature for at least one year. Her recipes had been collected over several years' time, some of them handed down from her mother and grandmother.

She also had a book of ancient methods dating back to Greek and Roman times. Every so often, when making the brew, she tossed some of the ingredients listed into the newer recipes, although the result, as in this instance, were not always happy. Tosca, a firm mead scholar, had read that the cave dwellings of primitive stone-age men show them collecting honey from bee colonies with the assumption that water was added to produce a mixture that could be fermented by wild yeasts.

"What's that awful smell?" said a male voice at the open door. Thatch stood outside, his hands raised in mock horror.

"If you were a Druid," Tosca said, "I'd have you drink the metheglin I was trying to brew, and your poetry would be inspired forever. At least, that's what the Druids claimed."

Thatch had confided in her that he wrote poetry, felt shy about it, but had finally allowed her to read some. It was filled with reminiscences about his childhood on a Wyoming ranch.

"Dang," he said, "just as I was becoming so fond of your mead." Tosca snorted at his joke. "So what's this new stuff you're concocting?"

"It's a version of mead, so you won't like it either, but the neighbors will, I'm quite sure, although they won't be able to taste it for years. That's how long it needs to be at its best. I plan to leave several bottles here long after I have returned to London."

She told him it was made with honey and herbs, was quite a lot spicier than mead, and had often been used as a medicinal potion in the sixteenth and seventeenth centuries.

"Metheglin was made even earlier, before the Romans invaded Britain, as a drink for warriors, and it was a drink made by witches. So you see, it's ancient. But J.J. has thrown away the Chinese herbs I bought," she said, frowning, "so I'll have to start all over again. Just as well, I suppose. I had no idea what I was buying, but the saleslady assured me the herbs were for vigor. Maybe I can order the elderflowers I need from home. Come in, I'll make coffee. Does it still smell bad?"

"Only enough to curl my toes. I see you're trying to air out the house. Let's go to the Coffee Can. You can tell me about metheglin, which sounds like one of your Cornish cuss words, and I'll tell you what I'm doing to find Sunida. I figured I'd better come straight over."

"Ah, The Woman and the Mystery of the Chandelier. Not a bad book title."

Fifteen

The day after her party Karma drove the two miles to Sheldon Hospital, hailed as one of the One Hundred Great Hospitals in America, an imposing multi-story building that stood on the bluffs in Newport Beach. She found a spot in the self-parking section for her truck, grumbling to herself about the newly implemented parking program, and wondering how many times she'd have to come here before Sally's death no longer required her attention. A parking rate sign declared that long-term passes were available for an annual cost of nine hundred dollars. At least I won't need one of those, Karma thought as she found her way to the lobby inside the hospital's main entrance. At the Information Desk she asked to see someone regarding a patient, Sally Hirsch.

"She's dead," Karma said. "Poor woman," she added at the receptionist's disapproving expression at her bald statement.

The receptionist made a phone call, directed Karma to a bank of elevators and told her to get off at the fifth floor. Soon seated opposite a charge nurse in a small room, Karma felt herself becoming anxious, wanting the meeting to be over as quickly as possible.

"Did she have any relatives, Miss Sanderson? Whom should we notify?"

Karma shrugged. "No one, as far as I know. She was around age seventy-two, and I never heard her talk about parents or siblings or any other family. She wasn't married and I guess had no children. We weren't that close. It just so happened she collapsed in my house."

"Would you be the person responsible for any financial debt?"

"No, of course not."

Karma almost laughed at the question. Her bank balance was so low she couldn't face even reading her monthly statement. It was definitely no concern of hers what happened to Sally's body, she thought. Damned nuisance she'd had the seizure at her house, and what a pity the woman hadn't left early, as she'd said she was going to when I invited her. What was it she'd said, that she didn't want to see Graydon Blair again if she could help it after the big quarrel they'd had the other day? Come to think of it, though, it was Oliver who'd started the argument.

At least from today onward she was free of Sally. After a lifetime of bickering over grandfather's contracts and the continual tension about his royalties with both Sally and Blair, Karma would now own the rights to all of Fuller's books. If I can get a lot of publicity about the lost manuscript being found, she thought, and with Swenson's help, we can start cashing in by getting a big publisher. Things are looking up, just as we planned.

It was common knowledge that Hirsch House was a one-man band run by Sally for the past eight years and was on the verge of bankruptcy. Sanderson had been her last big author whose books were considered classics. Karma had been trying without success for years to get the rights back to his works. Maybe she could begin building the Fuller Sanderson Library sooner than she'd expected.

"Miss Sanderson, you do know there's going to be an autopsy?" said the charge nurse, consulting her files.

"What?"

"Her cardiac arrest was unexpected, and the attending physician was uncomfortable with the manner of death. Soon after you left last night he notified the medical examiner. It's standard procedure in cases like this. Her body is now at the Santa Ana morgue. We can let you know the results, and perhaps you could arrange for a funeral home to pick the remains up after the authorities are finished with their investigation."

"What investigation?"

"As we always do in such cases, we'll be turning over to the police all the necessary materials, such as the death certificate, the autopsy report and the toxicology test results. Then you may claim the body.'

"Look, Miss Hirsch was just a business associate," Karma said. "Why should I be responsible for her?"

For a few seconds Karma enjoyed the thought of having Sally cremated and sprinkling the ashes on her compost heap. Kind of poetic justice since Karma was convinced she'd cheated her of thousands of dollars in royalties.

"Miss Sanderson?"

"Oh, sorry. I was just trying to figure out the kindest way to treat dear Miss Hirsch's remains even though I barely knew her. I suppose I could get in touch with the morgue and make the arrangements if I have to. As I said, I don't know much about her business or her personal life, and right now I have to get back to work."

"Understandable. It will probably take a while for the autopsy results, as the morgue is really backed up, although in some cases there are priorities. In the meantime, let me know if there is any assistance we can provide."

The charge nurse rose from her chair and walked with Karma to the elevator, expressing condolences.

Karma returned to the garden center, her mind racing. Sally's death opened up all kinds of convenient possibilities, the most important of which was that now Karma held all the cards for the ownership of her grandfather's books. Sally's death meant there'd be a reversion of rights, in this case to the author's heir, herself. Then there were the last, lost writings of Fuller Sanderson to be handled.

She'd fire Graydon Blair, of course, when it was all over. She should have done it years ago, when her parents died, but she'd been focused on building up her garden business. She'd no longer have to pay Blair fifteen percent of the royalties, not that they amounted to much these days, but now, with control in her own hands, Blair would soon be out of the picture. Who needs a literary agent when Fuller Sanderson is such a famous name? Well, it used to be, but I sure don't need that pretentious Blair, she decided.

"Hey, Karma, them cats are still mean. I told you that yesterday." Sam's voice pulled her out of her reverie. "What's that the humane shelter calls 'em? Special needs cats? Don't know why you ever adopted 'em. They don't even catch field mice. Why d'ya let 'em run all over?"

"Don't you dare touch them! It's not their fault they're arthritic. Running all over? They can barely walk, Sam, so stop complaining."

Karma stooped down under the desk and picked up one of the two sleeping tabby cats, stroking it gently. Her peevish expression softened as she bent her cheek to the cat's head and nuzzled it.

"Yeah, well," said Sam. "I don't care how cute you think they are, they sure have sharp teeth, and those claws work just fine. Look where they scratched me."

He pulled up the sleeve of his denim shirt to reveal three deep, bloody parallel red lines on his left arm.

"I've had far worse," said Karma. "Just make sure you put a bandage on those scratches before you go weeding in the giant milkweed patch again. I have told you several times that if any of the sap oozes out, or if you cut the stem by mistake, it's toxic."

"Wait a minute, I already got a rash from those plants. Look!"

Sam held out both hands, palms down. On the back of each hand was a small pink rash.

"Oh, Sam, don't be such a baby. It's nothing."

Sixteen

As Tosca was about to insert the flash drive into the laptop, excited to find out what was on it, she heard heavy footsteps coming up the outside steps. She quickly shut down the computer and went to the front door, where the top half was open. She knew it wasn't Thatch, because he'd gone out fishing on a friend's boat. When she recognized her visitor, she suppressed a groan. What's he doing here? she wondered.

"Morning, Mrs. Trevant. Sorry to bother you. May I come in?"

Newport Beach Homicide Detective Wally Parnell's expression and tone indicated he'd rather be anywhere else than inside her house. A man in his mid-forties, balding, with a trim physique, his long face reminded Tosca, fittingly, of a bloodhound.

"Come in, Chief Superintendent—oh, sorry, Detective. What brings you to the island again? Been quite a while since our last meeting," she said, grinning when he winced.

They had not parted on the best of terms during the time Parnell was investigating a murder on Isabel Island, and Tosca had been able to discover the killer.

"Are you collecting for the Police Benevolent Fund? I'm very happy to contribute."

"No, ma'am. We're interviewing everyone who was at Miss Sanderson's party, and I'd like to ask you some questions."

"Really? If Karma is complaining about the way we cleaned her house afterwards, well, then that's not very nice of her. I loathe housework, but it seemed the only charitable thing to do."

"It concerns Miss Sally Hirsch's death."

"That's interesting. How can I help you? I'd never met her before the party, but I knew she'd been Fuller Sanderson's publisher for years and years. We were all sad to hear she died. Oh, now I know exactly why you're here. It's about her purse, isn't it? Well, I haven't stolen it, if that's what you're thinking."

"No, ma'am. Miss Hirsch's purse has been recovered from Miss Sanderson. She brought it into the station yesterday. It's the manner of Miss Hirsch's death that we are investigating."

Tosca sensed at once that the detective's visit was to be not only an interesting one that set her curiosity meter soaring, but also lengthy, if she could keep him talking long enough. She plugged in the electric kettle and asked him if he'd like tea or mead. He declined both. While he fidgeted on the sofa with his notepad, she made herself a pot of PG Tips black tea, thinking she really must try to find some Yorkshire Gold. She heard it worked best in hard water areas like Newport Beach. The kettle soon boiled, and she warmed the pot with a little hot water, poured it out, spooned the tea leaves into the teapot and left it on the kitchen counter to brew.

"What do you mean, manner of death? It was epilepsy, wasn't it?" she said.

"Unfortunately not. Miss Hirsch might have been able to recover from such an episode. No. The preliminary autopsy states that her death was unnatural. She was poisoned."

"Poisoned? *Re'em fay!*" Tosca's swear word burst through her lips like a cheer, for which she instantly apologized.

"That's all right, Mrs. Trevant. I don't understand your language, and I'm sure my news is a shock to you. But it's kind of strange that the last time I was here in your house it turned out that the murder weapon was also poison. Coincidence?"

"Surely you are not suggesting I poisoned Sally? Besides, I caught the killer for you back then, remember?"

And now, she thought, I'm going to be on the trail of another one. She practically hugged herself before feeling guilty and silently saying, "Poor woman," to herself. Then, just as quickly, she hoped that if she solved the crime, it would mean her promotion to criminal reporter and return to the U.K. were in the bag.

"What kind of poison?" she said.

"The lab report says it is calotropin. It's more toxic than strychnine."

"Never heard of it, Inspector. Where can you buy it? Where does it come from? Is it a chemical? Can it be made into an insecticide?"

"Mrs. Trevant, I can tell you that it can be derived from the sap of the giant milkweed. I understand that Miss Sanderson planted some of those plants in six homeowners' yards here on the island. We'll be talking to them, of course. I don't see your name on that list, but you were one of the guests at her party, correct?"

"Yes, indeed, I was. The music was exceptional. Have you ever seen a theremin? However, I am sure you are busy and need to get on your way." She stood up, anxious for him to leave so she could research calotropin on the Internet. "Unless you'd like me to help you interview those six homeowners?"

Parnell squirmed. "No. We thank you for helping us out before, but I've got it covered. Now, if you don't mind, please sit down, and I'll get on with the questions. As I said, we're talking to everyone who attended the party."

Mind? Tosca could barely conceal her eagerness. What luck! She sat.

"Mr. Parnell, can you tell me more about the poison? How was it administered? Is it sticky stuff? Was it added to the *hors d'oeuvres*? Goodness, I ate several of them, mostly the tiny quiches. Why do you think I know anything? Sorry, I tend to ask questions all at once. Drives Thatch crazy. I very much admire your expertise in these matters. If I knew more about the poison, I might be able to help you," she added, thinking fat chance, buddy.

Parnell flipped a few pages over in his notepad and began to read.

"Calotropin is like morphine, an alkaloid extracted from flowering plants commonly called milkweeds. The white sap is the poisonous part and is used in pesticides. A fatal dose for humans is not very large, and the symptoms resemble an epilepsy attack with convulsions and vomiting."

"Of course! So that's what it really was, not epilepsy. Very Agatha Christie, although she much preferred her killers to use arsenic. Yes, Chief Superintendent, we all saw Sally convulsing, but she certainly didn't throw up. The only mess on the carpet was the drink she spilled as she fell, and we tried to clean it up as best we could."

"That was unfortunate," Parnell said, frowning at her, "because you removed much of that evidence, Mrs. Trevant. Thankfully, forensics was able to get enough of a sample for testing, and the result was that they found the calotropin. Now, I know you are keen on gardening, Mrs. Trevant. I wondered if you have seen anyone collecting sap from their milkweed plants."

Don't be daft, she wanted to reply but instead said, "No, of course I haven't. Who'd know enough to do that? Many of the islanders use Karma Sanderson's landscape service. She's here all the time and lives here, as you know. How is the sap collected?"

"All I want to know, Mrs. Trevant, is if you have seen your neighbors who have the plants in their yards doing anything suspicious, as I know you like to, um, observe things."

"You mean have I ever seen anyone going around with a little cup and collecting it like maple syrup? You say the sap is used in pesticides. I think strychnine is in rat poison, but I didn't know about calotropin. How fascinating."

"Yes, now, while you've been digging around in your neighbors' yards and fixing their plants, as I'm sure you have, did you notice if they had sprinkled any rat poison powder or other insecticide in the flower beds?"

"Me?" Tosca's euphoria at the prospect of having another murder to solve gave way to outrage. "I haven't been in anyone's yard lately. Well, only a couple. People do allow their nasturtiums to grow too leggy, don't you think?"

She realized as soon as she said it that her remark was not appreciated. She watched Parnell's frown deepen and sought to repair the damage.

"You know, Constable, I haven't seen any rats around, but we are having a problem with ants lately. I can't imagine why they take the trouble to walk all the way upstairs to our kitchen, but they do. I'll show you what I use to persuade them that the neighbor's house would be far more hospitable."

She went to the cabinet under the sink and removed a tall can of ant killer. "As stated on the list of ingredients and the warning label, this is apt to be fatal, too. Let me read them to you. They include imipothrin and cypermethrin," she said, stumbling over the names. "Oh, besides ants it kills crickets, silverfish and spiders."

"I doubt anyone is going to spray their human victim with enough of this to murder them," said Parnell as Tosca saw him repress a smile. "It has to be ingested. Now please tell me your version of Sally's collapse at the party."

"My version? Don't be silly, Mr. Parnell. I saw only what others saw. There were lots of people around, and we'd all have the same version, as you call it."

"Where were you standing?"

"Behind some people. We were listening to the musicians, Karma and Graydon Blair, playing when one of the strings on her guitar broke. Then we heard someone scream. It's not my fault if someone gets murdered, and I happen to be in the vicinity."

"Seems to happen to you a lot. All right, thank you for your time," said Parnell, getting up and practically charging out the door. "Oh, here's my card."

"I still have your card from the last time we met on the Whittaker matter, remember?"

"Please call me if you think of anything useful to the investigation."

Seventeen

Parnell left, clattering down the steps as quickly as possible. Tosca was sure he was hoping she'd never contact him again. Their relationship had not been a happy one after she'd shown him how wrong he'd been about a previous case.

Tosca planned to begin her own investigating. Here was an opportunity, albeit a sad one, to solve a crime, write it up and go home. Surely her editor couldn't refuse her the promotion she would deserve.

She started her online search by finding several web sites about the poisonous plant, following the trail of the calotropis gigantean, commonly known as giant milkweed. She read that the toxins within the plant were similar to digitalis or digoxin, a common heart medication. While all parts of the plant were considered toxic, it was the milky sap that could induce abnormal heart rates, tremors and seizures. It contained chemicals that were considered steroidal heart poisons.

A site devoted to Hinduism warned in one of its forums that giant milkweed is extremely toxic, and if the stem is cut and the sap touches the skin, it can cause sores and ulcers. At her computer she Googled "giant milkweed" and read with mounting excitement more references to the plant than Parnell had mentioned. An article was posted on a Far Eastern website that welcomed readers to the "sacred world of Hinduism." The lead headline read, "Giant milkweed – VERY TOXIC!" Several people commented in response on the site, one writing, "High doses can kill, and the sap was used in infanticide." Another stated, "The sap was used as poison on arrows," and that, mixed with food, can poison human beings.

"How lovely," thought Tosca. "A naturally green method of murdering someone."

Another web site suggested logging on to the Pet Poison Helpline. Here, Tosca typed "poison and milkweed" into the search box, not expecting any information when she clicked on it. To her surprise three pages showed up, noting the plant was poisonous to cats and dogs. "The toxins within these plants are similar to digitalis or digoxin, a common heart medication used in both human and veterinary medicine. Even the water in a vase containing the giant milkweed has been reported to cause toxicosis. Clinical signs from ingestion include cardiovascular (e.g. abnormal heart rhythm and rate), electrolyte abnormalities (e.g. a life-threatening high potassium level) … tremors and seizures."

At the web site of the Institute of Food and Agricultural Sciences at a university in Florida, giant milkweed was discussed at length in an article by a horticulture agent whose specialty was tropical flowering trees. She noted that the plant, calotropis gigantean, originated in the Far East, including India, and that the milky sap was poisonous. A third article Tosca read claimed that a copious white sap flowed whenever stems were cut.

Yet another article caught her eye, "A Poisoner's Guide to Central Park." The writer claimed that enough poisons existed in New York's eight-hundred forty-three-acre park to threaten the health of every jogger. Tosca read avidly, confirming at other online sites that the white fluid was highly toxic and that one milkweed in the calotropis plant family was more lethal than strychnine. Even the water in a vase became lethal if giant milkweeds were placed in it.

The plants were grown in many countries and sometimes used to attract Monarch butterflies. Full sun was preferred.

"Hmm," she murmured, "dandy for growing in Southern California."

Then she remembered seeing the large glass case of butterflies in Karma's office. She hoped Sam was still at Karma's business. She picked up her cell phone, found the number and touched the screen to dial.

"Karma's Garden Center. Yeah?"

"Sam, this is Mrs. Trevant. I was there earlier today with my neighbor. I'm sorry to bother you again, but I wondered if you would mind taking a peek at Karma's butterfly collection and let me know if there are any Monarchs included?"

"Don't have to. There's a couple right here." He took the jar down from the shelf. "Caught 'em meself."

"Thank you."

She was about to hang up when he added, "Had dozens of Monarchs attracted to the giant milkweeds before she sold 'em to her customers. Kama likes to collect Monarchs, but I'm not a fan of butterflies. They're just winged worms, that's all. Good riddance, I say. Karma tole me that's why that publisher lady died. The cops said she was killed with the poison from the plant by drinking it. Ha!"

Tosca pulled her cell quickly away from her ear at the sound of Sam slamming his phone onto its receiver, speculating that Karma probably still used an old-fashioned phone in the office.

Sam's last remark sent Tosca's brain spinning. Someone had to have known the white milkweed sap was poisonous and added it to Sally's drink. It would have blended perfectly into Sally's creamy White Russian cocktail without being noticed. But I can't believe Karma would do such a thing, she thought. She's a lover of nature behind that brash manner of hers, and she takes in stray cats. The woman readily admits she's underwater financially, but surely she's not desperate enough to kill someone. Yet, who else but her would know that milkweed sap could be deadly? Was Karma coerced to murder Sally? And if so, by whom?

Sam said that Karma had planted the milkweeds in several yards on the island. Maybe one of the homeowners had a motive for killing Sally. Time to do some more investigating. But now she needed to explore the flash drive.

Eighteen

Still munching on toast and marmalade, Tosca sat in the dining nook and booted up her laptop, pleased that J.J. was planning to go out, leaving her alone. She didn't want any distraction from what she was convinced was an exciting find.

Tosca inserted the flash drive Arlene had found under the chair at Karma's house and waited for its Windows file directory to appear on the monitor. This time I'm going to study this file from beginning to end, she resolved, and see if it really is Sanderson's last book. If lengthy, it might mean all his notes are here, too, and probably several drafts of the same book.

Hmm, she reflected. If part of the long document is the lost manuscript Karma was talking about at the party, it made sense that Sally would have it, but why was she keeping it secret? Had she even told Karma she'd found it, if indeed she had? The anniversary celebration the other night would have been the perfect time to announce the discovery of Sanderson's lost manuscript. His granddaughter said they were still looking for it, yet here it was copied, Tosca assumed, from Sanderson's own handwriting or typewritten pages and certainly from a computer's hard drive. The question was, whose?

The more Tosca thought about the possibility of the treasure trove of an undiscovered work, the more eager she was to read every word. It would be the centerpiece of the new Sanderson Library that Karma planned to build.

J.J. interrupted Tosca's musings. "I'm off to the garage," she said, "then the track for practice. Will you be all right? What about the car?"

"All right? I'm not ready for a wheelchair yet. What do you mean, all right?"

"Now don't get your knickers in a twist, Mother. I just want to make sure you'll be okay here all day. And if you drive the Healey, please be gentle. Try not to grind the gears. It strips them."

"Yes, yes. It's not me that does the grinding, it's the car. We really should get rid of that old bucket. It doesn't like me, you know. Even when your father was alive and we'd go on outings, I always felt it wanted to chuck me out."

"Mother, stop being so melodramatic."

"Why do I always get the feeling our roles are reversed when you talk like that? Anyway, love, off you go, and enjoy your day."

While she waited for the Word program to appear, she filled and switched on the electric kettle, added a teabag to a Minton bone china tea cup and returned to the computer. A directory appeared, listing a single document with the simple heading, "Three."

Tosca clicked to open it and saw the words, Bright Purple Nights by Fuller Sanderson. A list of forty-six chapters followed. Did 'Three' refer to a subtitle? Familiar with all of the author's books, she knew this could be the last one he had written before his death and perhaps had never delivered to Hirsch House. Who had saved this document to the flash drive? It must belong to Hirsch House, though, so it was Sally's after all.

What a coup for my newspaper, she thought, if I could write a book review of this unpublished manuscript. It would appear in the *Daily Post Sunday Magazine*, which was much more prestigious than the daily paper.

Before hitting the Print button, she fast-forwarded to the final chapter, then pressed Enter to go to the next page in case he'd written notes and listed resource material. She had several author friends who kept jottings, questions, resources used for the plot, characters, settings and even musings at the end of their document, while others wrote them into the body of the work as it was written and played out. Tosca was a reader for two of her writer friends, dissecting their first drafts to see if all the elements hung together and each thread was tied up by the conclusion of the book. She disliked the job and found it time consuming, but friends were friends.

Tosca checked the document's word count. It was eighty-seven thousand words, about twenty thousand words longer than he usually wrote, she knew. All of his previous books were around sixty-five thousand, so it seemed there were indeed notes at the end, perhaps for even more books, including, she hoped, several synopses for future plots. That would make the document extremely valuable, because none of the drafts or notes for his earlier books existed.

However, instead of seeing any of Sanderson's notes at the end of the document or synopses for future books, she was faced with another title page: Seven Doors to Doom. A second book? Tosca checked the word count, which was eighty-five thousand, five hundred. Again, this was more than the author had ever previously written.

Mystified, she clicked on the down arrow to the final chapter, pressed Enter again and came upon yet another title page: Silver Blue Shadow. This third document had no chapters listed and appeared half finished. It ended abruptly in the middle of chapter seventeen. There were no further writings.

"What on earth is all this?" she asked aloud. "Two Sanderson books he never published and one in progress?"

Barely containing her excitement, she printed everything out, thanking her stars she'd bought five reams of copy paper for her laser printer the week before. When the machine finally stopped she collected the pages from the tray. Why had he written these books with far more words than usual? Here were close to two hundred fifty thousand for all three. Ideally, there shouldn't be more than one hundred eighty thousand words, but what a discovery!

Engrossed in trying to figure out the puzzle, Tosca was alerted by a harsh whistle. Steam was shooting out of the electric kettle's spout. She got up, poured some hot water into the teapot to warm it, swished it around, and poured the water out into the sink. This time, deciding she needed something special to celebrate her find, she spooned loose black Darjeeling tea into the pot, added hot water to the brim and put the lid on. She covered the teapot with a padded linen tea-cozy that had the words "St. Ives" embroidered all over it in knotwork and sat back down at the laptop.

Nineteen

Tosca studied the first manuscript and became fascinated by the new story as related by Sanderson's fictional detective, Johnny DiLeo. She chuckled as she followed the tale of murder and mayhem in old-time Hollywood, when movie stars were treated like possessions by the studios. But as she read she came across one or two anachronisms. Surely cars had no seatbelts back then? And Sanderson had changed DiLeo's eyes from blue to hazel. Tosca figured that the author's aging memory was probably the cause of the missteps, and the publisher's editors would have caught the mistakes before publication.

Familiar with the author's entire body of work, she knew these titles had never seen the light of day—at least, not commercially. As Tosca had told Arlene, Sanderson was her favorite crime writer, and she had not only read all his books but had studied his style and life. After she had read *The Total Surrender,* his most popular because of its exotic sex scenes set in Tahiti, she'd wanted to visit the island and go to all the locations the author mentioned, but life had intervened, or rather, J.J. had. At least now I'm living on an island, Tosca thought, and there's plenty of sun, sand and ocean, although far from the alluring South Seas that Somerset Maugham made famous with his stories.

The more she studied the books, the more she wondered why Sally and the others pretended they were looking for a single manuscript. Or were they pretending? There was no telling who the flash drive belonged to, as anyone at the party could have dropped it.

Tosca went into the kitchen to make another pot of tea, telling herself she could easily drown in tea if she didn't figure out the puzzle soon.

Sally must have known what was on the drive, of course, if it was hers, but she was dead. Karma, then? Yet, for some reason, Tosca hesitated. She liked the woman and didn't believe she'd get involved in what appeared to be some sort of nefarious scheme. Had another writer added to these unpublished books she'd found? It would be a world-wide sensation in the publishing industry, if so, and ruin Sanderson's reputation. Was that what the argument at the French restaurant had been about?

If the books were fakes, which one had planned the scheme? Of the four—Blair, Sally, Swenson and Karma—she'd put her money on Graydon Blair to be perpetrating the fraud. Or was he unaware of these manuscripts, and they were real? Yes, she'd better ask him first and sort it all out. After all, he was Sanderson's agent of record. If he had no idea they existed, he'd be thrilled that these works had been found, and he'd know exactly how to handle them.

The icing on the cake for Tosca would be the fact that she had made the discovery and would be able to write an article on how she solved the mystery for Karma. It was the sort of tabloid article she excelled at, a poverty-stricken, titian-haired young woman who was the heiress to a possible fortune through her famous grandfather and his long-lost manuscripts. If they were fakes, the story would be even more fascinating.

Satisfied with her decision, she returned the Darjeeling tea to its shelf and looked for the green and beige foil bag that contained her favorite loose leaf Yorkshire Gold. She'd discovered it while talking to a fellow author, Catriona

McPherson, who loved its rich malty flavor from a blend of thirty varieties from India, Africa, and Sri Lanka. The bag bore a photo of the English countryside, which reminded Tosca of home.

On second thought, she decided her discovery called for mead, the very special muscatel that had taken six months or more to mature before it was ready to drink. It had a seventeen percent alcohol content, but she didn't plan to drive anywhere. She was too absorbed in what she'd found.

The task of reading all three books took Tosca several hours, and by late afternoon she still had not finished. In order not to break her concentration, she stopped reading at four p.m. to toast more bread, spread it with coconut oil, her replacement for butter, and add dollops of marmalade. Fortified with yet another cup of tea, Tosca resumed reading.

By eight o'clock she was halfway into the final partial manuscript and completely absorbed when she was startled to hear the first ten notes of Mozart's "Symphony No. 40." It was the ringer on her cell phone. Grabbing it, she blurted out "*Jowl*," greeting the caller with the exclamation as the phone tumbled out of her grasp and fell to the floor face down. Tosca picked it up, saying into the speaker, "Terribly, terribly sorry. Let me try that again. Hello?"

Twenty

"*Jowl*? That's a new one on me."

"Oh, Thatch, it's you. Yes, you know I revert to my own language when I'm caught off guard. Anyway, I only said Damn."

"Because?"

"It's the most extraordinary thing. That flash drive Arlene found at Karma's house contains what I believe could be three unpublished Sanderson books, or at least two and a half books, and not the single manuscript that Karma said she was looking for."

"That should make her happy," said Thatch.

"On the other hand, they could be fakes."

"Can't you tell?"

"No," said Tosca. "They are identical to Sanderson's style. The only thing is, they are much longer than the books he wrote."

"I'm sure you'll figure it out, but before you bury your head into the mystery much longer, think about taking a drive down to San Diego with me."

"Oh, yes, I'd love to go. I've heard so much about the San Diego zoo. I hear visitors can comb a pygmy goat's hair and watch elephant husbandry training."

"Sorry, Tosca, not what I have in mind. Ever been digging for gemstones?"

"Of course not, although my great uncles were tin miners in Cornwall, so I suppose digging is in my blood. Besides working in the tin mines, they dug for clay, too, which makes excellent cat litter. Do I hear a snigger? Anyway, I hope we're not going to be digging up graves among the gems, are we?"

Thatch laughed. "Not this time. I thought you might want to check out the Chandelier tourmaline, Sally's gemstone that you took home. I told you how famous it is. It came from the Oceanview Mine north of San Diego. It's one of nine mineral mines in the area and the only fully operating one that allows the public to spend the day screening for local gemstones. I'm surprised you don't want to find out what Sally was doing with it since someone else's name was engraved on the silver base."

"Of course I want to find out. In fact, that is exactly what I planned to do myself. What kind of mine is it?"

"Minerals."

"You mean as in calcium and magnesium? I take both of those supplements every day."

"No, no, not the kind you eat." He smiled. "I'm talking about aquamarine, kunzite, garnets, crystal, quartz and, of course, tourmaline in all different colors of the rainbow. There have been some spectacular finds in the San Diego area, which is known among gemologists as the Big Kahuna."

Thatch reminded her that the Chandelier's twin, the Candelabra, was found at the mine right across from the Oceanview Mine.

"I'm sold. Be ready in a jiffy." Tosca hoped Thatch would appreciate her brisk, brief reply in deference to his own style of talking.

"How long is a jiffy in Cornwall-speak?" he said. "But we can't go today, it's too late. I need time to fill out the mine's liability form for us both and make reservations, so we'll have to wait until tomorrow. You'll need to bring gloves and a hat and be prepared to get dusty. We'll be spending the entire day down there."

"All day down a mine? Exactly how much digging will we have to do?"

She mentally envisioned herself with a flickering miner's lamp strapped to her head, shovel in hand, covered in coal dust, and timbers falling all around as the roof caved in.

"No, by down there I mean traveling south to the San Diego area."

"It's not that hot Anza-Borrego Desert, is it? That was south of here, too."

"This time we'll be up in the mountains. You'll love it."

"That's what you promised last time, and before we'd even had lunch we'd dug up a body."

"I can go alone, then, if you prefer. I know the mine owner, and I'd like to see him again as well as see if he's found any more large tourmalines like the one Sally had."

"Don't you dare leave me out. What time tomorrow?"

"Dawn." At her gasp Thatch added, "Okay, 8:00 a.m. Oh, you still have the Chandelier, right?"

"Yes, I was going to give it back to Karma today."

"Hold on to it for a little while longer. We need to take it with us to the mine."

"All right. *Kosk ya ta, keresik.*"

"That's a new one, although I've heard the last word before."

"It's really easy to understand. It just means 'Sleep well, Darling.'"

She was still smiling when she pressed the red circle on the screen to close the call, not quite sure if she'd hung up or not. Her new iPhone5 had so many features she wasn't always sure she'd closed down, signed off, hit the correct button, deleted the entire phone directory or ruined it in some way forever.

At 10:00 p.m. she went to bed, her head buzzing with the discovery of the Sanderson manuscripts and their meaning to the publishing industry and to Sanderson fans. She was still trying to solve the puzzle of his decision to write far more than his usual word count, if indeed he did, as she drifted off to sleep.

Twenty-One

At almost eight o'clock the next morning Thatch climbed into his battered silver pickup truck, a survivor of his many off-road geological expeditions, to make the short trip to Isabel Island from his hillside house in Upper Newport Bay. The steep white bluffs below his house bordered the Santa Ana River that had carved out a canyon to form the bay and mingle with the ocean-fed harbor below.

He was always grateful to have found a home that was set back and high up, far removed from the bustle of the hundreds of yachts that sat at anchor below, music blaring from a few decks and the buzz of mechanical equipment as owners worked on their boats. On a good day he could see Santa Catalina Island, twenty-five miles to the west. For years before she died his wife had urged him to buy a boat so they could visit more often instead of having to take the catamaran ferry over, but he never took to owning a boat.

Thatch's quiet location also overlooked the several habitats in an ecological reserve with mud flats and a saltwater marsh. Home to wildlife and until a few years ago to a variety of birds, including loons, grebes, bufflehead, eared and pied-billed stoters, and mergansers, the area was under threat due to erosion and development. One part of the cliffs had already been ruined, in his opinion, by a row of thirty identical luxury homes built on a summit, all painted white, resembling a row of outsize teeth.

Nevertheless, migrating birds flew in for brief stopovers on their way elsewhere, and Thatch enjoyed watching their activities. As an amateur geologist, a hobby he'd turned to after retiring a year earlier as an agent with the U.S. Secret Service, he liked poking around the estuary, chipping carefully away at the small rocks, inspecting the silt carried down from the north and studying the strata in the tall cliffs that rose to one hundred feet from sea level to a flat mesa.

Thatch took his time on his way to pick up Tosca, enjoying the smell of the sea air and anticipating the pleasure of her company for the entire day. He knew there was a mutual attraction between them but recognized she was a prize he had to be careful not to lose by coming on too strongly as a brash American. He had learned by now that Tosca, despite her erratic impulsiveness, was one shrewd lady and the most honest woman about expressing herself he'd ever met, even if sometimes she appeared naïve.

He told himself she hadn't had much experience with rodeo riders from Wyoming and certainly not with a former secret agent. He liked to imagine her having tea every day with the Queen, although he knew it wasn't true. Tosca told him she'd found the gossip for her newspaper column mainly through her friendship with the hundreds of maids, butlers and other staff who served the royal family, and definitely not with the royals themselves.

Thatch approached the bridge onto Isabel Island, as always enthralled by the quaint cottages and over-the-top mansions that crowded into its three miles. Considered the jewel of the city of Newport Beach, the island's residential streets lived up to its reputation by naming them for gemstones with signs for amethyst, topaz, agate, opal, onyx and others. The only commercial street, Moonstone, was crammed with storefront art galleries, boutiques, tiny but chic restaurants and a tavern. The street ended at the bay front where the ferry, an old barge, carried three cars, bicycles and dozens of passengers between the island and the peninsula that linked up to Newport Beach at its northeast end.

Reflecting on how the island had evolved from a quaint little beach community built on a sandbar to a sophisticated all-year resort where sleekly toned women jogged in Chanel sweat suits and shopped in Ferragamo shoes, he chuckled at a saying he'd heard that in Newport Beach it was a bigger sin to be fat than financially unethical.

Tosca and J.J. were standing on the sidewalk when he arrived on Fenton Street. He found a free spot, parked and jumped out of the driver's seat.

"Are you coming with us?" He noticed J.J. held no racing helmet in her hand.

"No," interrupted Tosca. "She's waiting for a ride to pick up your daughter. You gave J.J. permission the other day, remember? They are going to visit a couple of retirement homes," said Tosca.

At Thatch's puzzled expression J.J. quickly explained, "No, not for you or my mother, although I think people should plan ahead." Tosca rolled her eyes as J.J. continued, "It's just that I found out something interesting that isn't gossip or crime related, for a change. There's a new program with a musical connection that appeals to me. As you know, I can't stand opera, even though our family boasts of two divas and a tenor, and I have to tell mother to pipe down when she gets the urge to sing those high notes around here." She gave Tosca a hug. "Anyway, I heard about a music program that can unlock memories in Alzheimer's patients. The father of one of my racing buddies is in a care home where they have just started the program. He told me about it, and he's just added their logo to the side of his race car."

"Is it a sing-a-long?" said Thatch.

"No, nothing like that. The patients are provided with iPods and headphones," she said, "and they are invited to select their favorite music from their past, the kind they listened and danced to as teenagers. I'll know more after my visit. Oh, here's my ride."

A candy-apple red 1964 convertible Mustang slid alongside Thatch's truck. J.J. ran over to the car, waved goodbye and got in. The driver smiled at Thatch and Tosca and roared off down the one-way street. They watched it turn the corner and disappear.

Thatch opened the passenger side door of his truck. "Okay, so it's not a snazzy, sexy machine like the Mustang," he said to Tosca as he helped her climb up onto the seat, "but I like my workhorse."

He patted the door after closing it, went around to the driver's side and eased onto the worn vinyl. He handed Tosca a map, pages of pictures and text he'd downloaded from the mineral mine's web site, and his Garmin GPS device.

"I've set it to take us to the mine," said Thatch. "It's been quite a while since I was in that area, which is pretty desolate. The roads can flood or be blocked by a mudslide. If so, the Garmin can lead us to detours."

"Why do you always find such unpleasant places for me to endure?"

"Aren't you my hardy Cornishwoman, used to struggling over those wild, windy moors?" said Thatch, grinning.

Twenty-Two

Thatch slid the truck into gear, and they left Isabel Island to head for the Interstate 5 South. As they passed Camp Pendleton Marine Base, Tosca looked for the resident buffalo and horses.

"I've never even caught so much as a glimpse of those animals you told me live on this land," she complained.

"The bison are there, all right, but not near the freeways. The camp goes back many miles." His words were almost drowned out by two teams of military helicopters droning overhead on a training mission as they flew toward the beach. "Looks like the Marines are practicing landings for more deployment to the Middle East."

He craned his neck to glance up through the top of the windshield as the noise increased tenfold. "Whoa! Military warplanes. First time I've seen them out here. That's extraordinary."

"Why?"

"We usually see helicopter pilots training at this marine base, not war planes." They were silent for several miles, Tosca feeling blessed that J.J. had chosen a civilian career despite its dangers on the race track.

Thatch left the freeway at Route 79 South, then took Route 76 East. As they passed vineyards and wineries, Tosca expressed her surprise, saying she thought all California wines came from Napa and Sonoma in Northern California.

"As a matter of fact," said Thatch, "this area here, Temecula Valley, has more than two dozen wineries. We could take a tour sometime."

"All right, as soon as I solve Sally's murder."

Two huge color billboards advertising the Pechanga Casino came into view with photos of the resort and casino, showing its warm adobe exterior, and touting its live concerts.

"Should we stop and try our luck?" she said. "It looks inviting."

"Nope. We're still thirty miles from the mine. The Pechanga is the biggest casino in California built by the Pechanga tribe. Don't worry, there's another casino at the foot of a mountain where the mine is. It's the marker for the turn-off to Oceanview."

Tosca was humming "Musetta's Waltz Song" from one of her favorite operas, *La Boheme*, when she saw a large, slab-sided red brick building. "Oh, there's the casino. How ugly! What was the architect thinking?"

Thatch smiled. "That's the power station, honey. Look up ahead to the right. That's the casino."

Situated alone in the midst of vacant fields, the massive three-tiered, ten-story palace rose up from its location on the Pala Indian Reservation like an ancient temple arising from the sea. Imposing by its sheer size, the casino was half-moon shaped and dominated the landscape.

"It's bigger than Buckingham Palace!" said Tosca.

"Like the design? It was inspired by Frank Lloyd Wright's philosophy of planning structures to be organic and in harmony with humanity."

"That sounds poetic, though I doubt you've written a poem about his buildings. In any case I don't see the connection," she said. "It's rather stark standing there, but yes, it is magnificent. Are we going in?"

"Nope. Here's our turnoff. We're not far from the entrance to the property where the mine is located."

Thatch took the small lane to the left. After driving a couple of miles uphill the paved road turned into a rutted dirt trail with orange and tangerine groves crowding in from each side. A sign warned that the land was private property.

"Fiddle," said Tosca, "I was hoping to pick a few oranges."

"There's a fruit stand near the Pala casino, Tosca. We can stop there on the way home."

"You're no fun, Mr. Wyoming."

Twenty-Three

A mile farther on they saw a driver in a large golf cart, waiting outside a chain link fence, the gate of which was open. The driver introduced himself as Tom and told Thatch and the three other people already waiting there to follow him in their cars.

The caravan of vehicles, two of them SUVs, followed the golf cart up the mountain after Tom paused to close and padlock the gate. Tosca looked eagerly around as the trees and brush fell away to reveal a series of surrounding mountains.

They finally reached a plateau and followed directions about where to park. Tosca made sure she had her parasol, a large-brimmed hat, gloves and a canvas bag containing the box with the Chandelier tourmaline when she got out of the truck. Thatch retrieved two small red coolers from the truck bed.

"Lunch," he explained,

Part of the mountainside had been sliced off to form a large circle containing fifty small, sturdy wooden tables, half already occupied by eager diggers. On each table were a wooden sifting screen placed over a tub of water, a trowel and a bucket. In the middle of the area was a twelve-foot-high pile of gravel. Off to one side was a shaded picnic patio with tables and benches.

"Tailings again?" said Tosca, pointing at the pile. "You said we were going to find gems, not dig through a ton of pebbles like we did in the Anza-Borrego Desert before finding that poor boy's grave."

"Calm down, Tosca. No need to get all riled up. That's where the gemstones are, right there in the pile. You just have to sift through and pick them out. But first let's go find Jeff Stanger, the owner of the mine, and ask him about the Chandelier."

The driver told them to choose a table they'd like to work at, and that he'd be back in half an hour to begin a talk on how to screen for gems.

Thatch saw that the mine owner had spotted him and was walking toward him, hand outstretched, a big grin on his rugged, weathered face.

"Hey, Thatch, been a long time. And who's this pretty lady?"

Thatch introduced Tosca, who took the box containing the Chandelier tourmaline from her tote bag and opened it.

"Good lord," said Stanger, a look of wonder on his face. "Where did you come across this? It's our mine's most famous piece, a true treasure and almost priceless." He removed the Chandelier from its box. "I'm sure you know this is the twin to the Queen Mine's Candelabra. I can't believe I'm holding it. It was sold way before my time."

He turned the gem around and around as Thatch had done when he first held it in Karma's living room. Tosca was amused by the obvious thrill Stanger took in inspecting it. "Look at the depth of color," he said, "the striations, the ... Did you buy it?"

"No, Jeff, we're trying to find the owner," said Thatch. "There's an engraving on it." He indicated the name on the silver base. "Do you know who this Sunida is?"

"Man, that was many, many years ago. I don't know if the previous owner even left a file on it. No one's seen it for decades, and I was told the buyer insisted on privacy. We might have something. Let me check it out in my office.

While I do that, why don't you two grab a table and equipment and join in the fun? Tom's about to start his spiel." Stanger strode over to a motor home and went inside.

Thatch turned to Tosca. "I'll get the coolers and put them in the shade."

"I'll help you."

They set the coolers on the ground in the lunch area, then found an empty screening table and listened to the mining expert give instructions to the diggers, explaining how to fill their buckets from the tailings pile, the way to handle the washing, screening and sifting process, and what to look for. He held up different gems to show their colors and noted that some minerals of the same kind can be black, green, pink or white.

"When they're washed off, you'll be surprised by their colors," Tom said.

He finished his talk by telling everyone to bring their buckets and trowels to the tailings pile and take only half a load, because a full one would be very heavy. Tosca gingerly approached the mound and walked all around it.

"No gems here," she muttered to Thatch at her side, "just a pile of small grey stones. Looks like a rubbish heap."

"Wrong. There's a piece of black quartz, see it?" He picked out a tiny dark pebble.

"It's microscopic, grey and full of dust."

"Wait till you've washed it, you'll be surprised. Want me to fill the bucket for you?"

"Of course not. Thanks, but I can handle it myself."

She moved away, dug into the pile and shoveled the haul into the bucket. Thatch did the same, grinning all the way back to their table.

Tosca emptied the contents of her bucket onto the screening tray, which was sitting above a pan of water, lowered it and moved the screen as instructed from left to right, washing the sand and silt off. Thatch helped her pick out the likeliest pieces to be of interest, naming each one.

"Oh, my goodness," she said. "Is this an emerald?"

Twenty-Four

"Sorry, honey, that's green mica. There's no chromium in this soil, which is what emeralds need, but look at this quartz crystal, it's beautiful. It'd make a nice pendant."

Thatch handed her a one-inch stone covered in clay.

"Wash it, and you'll see how pretty it is. It's white under all the dirt."

"Thank you." She placed the gemstone in her screen that contained some of the tailings she hadn't yet cleaned, lowered it into the pan of water and again moved the screen from side to side before raising it. She picked up the crystal, exclaiming, "You're right, it is a beautiful little piece. What luck!"

Her enthusiasm for going over to the pile and filling her bucket again increased. Thatch advised her to search for pieces with vertical striations and any that looked like small sticks of candy or pencils.

After they had filled their buckets twice more and repeated the process of washing and sifting, Bill announced a break for lunch, and everyone went over to the patio area and their coolers.

"What did you bring to eat?" said Tosca.

"Cornish pasties."

"No! Where did you find them?"

"At an Indian grocery store in Irvine. They were frozen, but they're made and imported from jolly old England. I heated them up before we left, so they should still be warm."

"Probably been frozen for years, but I appreciate the thought. Let's give them a try."

She unwrapped one and bit into the pie crust, which was shaped in a half-circle and fluted at the edges. Gravy, peas and small pieces of meat and potatoes spurted out onto the picnic table, missing Tosca's T-shirt by inches.

"Wonderful!" She pronounced the pasties as close to perfect as she'd ever tasted and asked Thatch for the grocery store's address, adding, "Of course, not quite as good as Mr. Kernow's shop in St. Ives, but very, very close."

As they finished lunch Stanger, waving a slim envelope, called out to Thatch and Tosca to join him in the motor home.

"Hey, I'm glad I was able to find this," he said when they were inside. "It was in an old file folder I hadn't opened in years. Guy by the name of Norman Sanderson bought the Chandelier from this mine three decades ago, according to the receipt, and had it hand delivered to a Sunida Sittikul in Laguna Beach. Is that any help?"

Tosca whooped with delight. "Our mystery woman who's connected to our case! This gets better and better."

Thatch was more reserved. "Calm down, honey. Don't go jumping to your usual conclusions here. Jeff, is there an address?"

"Yep. I guess it's okay to give it to you."

Stanger opened the envelope, extracted a receipt, copied the address down on a piece of paper and handed it to Thatch.

"I'd be interested to hear more about this when you've found the owner," said Stanger. "Oh, by the way, let me show you a couple of other great pieces we found. I know you'll appreciate them, Thatch."

He went to the back and returned with a crystal the size of a large baking potato, explaining it was the biggest, most lustrous and colorful dark kunzite yet extracted from one of the pockets in the mine.

"And here's a classic smoky quartz on microcline," he said, holding out a palm-sized, two-toned, light and dark green gemstone that glittered in the sun.

At Tosca's puzzled expression Thatch explained that microcline was a mixture of minerals that share the same chemistry but have different crystal structures.

"It's a semi-precious stone and often pink, brown or green. Many of them are translucent, like this one," he said.

They exchanged a few more pleasantries with Stanger and left, Tosca clutching both the box and the paper with the address. Thatch carried a small plastic bag half-filled with the small pieces of black, aquamarine, pink and crystal gems they had found in their buckets.

"Here, Tosca, these are for you," he said, handing her the bag after they got into the truck. "Not worth much, but since we can take home anything we find at no cost, you should keep them as a reminder of your mining experience. It wasn't so bad, was it? Besides, these gems were dug with love."

"All right, thank you. I could put them in the bottom of an aquarium, if I had one. But 'dug with love?' How elegantly poetic." Her grin softened the sarcasm as she took the bag.

"If you don't like dug with love, how about, 'the poetry of the earth is never dead'?"

"Did you just make that up?" said Tosca

"Keats."

"What's the poem called?"

"The title is 'On the Grasshopper and Cricket.' The context is wrong for the meaning I want to convey about our time today, but I couldn't resist," he said. "Keats was referring to how the grasshopper keeps his song alive during scorching summers, and the cricket's song does the same for the bitter winters, ensuring that the poetry of the earth never dies."

"That is truly beautiful. I don't know much about Keats, except that he was a romantic, short in stature, and died young while living in Rome. Oh, I see some oranges fallen from that tree. Shall we stop and get them?"

In response Thatch increased his speed down the mountain despite the hazardous ruts in the trail.

"No trespassing means just that, so no, we are not stopping. I'll buy you some."

"Don't bother, Thatch. It's just that forbidden fruit always tastes sweeter."

He didn't reply, and Tosca began to speculate on Sunida's identity.

Twenty-Five

"Could she be an illegitimate daughter of Fuller's? A long-lost sister? A secret wife? At least she lives near us in Laguna Beach," Tosca said, reading the address aloud. "But what a strange last name."

"Not strange at all," said Thatch, slowing down at each sharp bend as they descended the mountain. "Sounds typically Thai to me."

"Thai? How do you figure that? Ah, you are fluent in the language, I suppose," she said, clearly in disbelief.

"No, but I learned a few words when working security for a U.S. president and his wife on their state visit to Bangkok. One of the Thai reporters, a beautiful young woman, at the press conference had a similar name."

"Oops. I am suitably admonished."

"There you go again, going all formal on me."

They reached the bottom of the mountain. Tosca stared once again at the huge Pala casino before Thatch turned the truck to the right to head back to Isabel Island.

"Tell me more about the beautiful tourmaline and its twin," said Tosca, "if you can bear to utter more than a few words." She punched him playfully on the shoulder.

"I can talk your ear off about rocks and stones, and I know a little about mineral mining," he said, "which I learned from Jeff."

Thatch told her he'd first met Stanger at a gem show where booths were laden with dazzling minerals and natural gemstones of every hue. The Oceanview booth had as its centerpiece a framed poster-sized, full-color photo of the blazing pink tourmaline crystal that came to be called the Chandelier. One of the largest and its most renowned find since the mine opened in 1907, the tourmaline was famous for its three pipes that resemble holders for tiny candles, although that is equally true of the Candelabra.

"The Chandelier's various shades of pink, lavender and mauve are magnificent," said Thatch. "I was instantly smitten and began going to the local mineral mines for digs. It's great fun, and a day up in these mountains is a pleasure. It's an active mine and one of the few that allows the public to spend a day digging."

"Did you ever find any wonderful gems?" said Tosca.

"Nope. Some chips of black tourmaline, a chunk of aquamarine, and a few pieces of kunzite, but nothing that was worth much in terms of money. To me, it's the anticipation, the discovery, not the end result that counts. Plenty of amateurs come here, some regularly, hoping for a big payday. Did I tell you about the Empress of China?"

"Is that another great find? A piece of tourmaline like the Chandelier?"

Thatch let out a hearty bellow and shook his head. He took his right hand off the steering wheel and patted Tosca's thigh.

"Sorry," he said, "but I can see why you would think so. No, she was a real person."

He told her of a legend, that the last Empress of China, Tzu Hsi, had a passion for pink and red gems. In the early 1900s tourmalines in various colors were being found in the Big Kahuna Zone around Pala mines. Tiffany and other American jewelers sold the crystals for carving to local Chinese jewelers. When the Empress saw the bracelets and necklaces brought to her in China, she fell in love with them and sent her people to the Pala mines to buy up vast quantities of the gemstones. She loved every variation of the color pink and had it fashioned into jewelry, embedded into custom-made ceramic dishes and even into a stone pillow she was said to sleep on.

"What a fascinating story," said Tosca. "Do the Chinese still buy from the mines?

"I doubt it after China became Communist, and luxury was prohibited."

"Yes, of course, I forgot, although these days the rich Chinese are buying tons of American real estate. Oh, we're almost home. What a splendid day we've had. Wait till I show these gems to J.J.," she said, rattling the small plastic bag Thatch had given her.

They crossed the narrow bridge onto Isabel Island, and Thatch stopped his truck in front of Tosca's house. As she alighted, prepared to invite Thatch in for a nightcap, she paused and held up her hand.

"Listen. Do you hear that?"

"Music." Thatch shrugged.

"Not just music, *keresik*. It's 'Greensleeves' and being played on a spinet, no less, the instrument it was originally written for."

She looked up and down the street.

"Is that significant?" said Thatch, following her as she began to walk toward the sound. "It's a beautiful composition, by the way, but not one of your operas, I'd bet."

"Then you'd be wrong," she retorted. "It's from Ferrucio Busoni's short opera *Turandot*. He incorporated into it a ballad called 'Greensleeves.' The piece was originally a medieval folk song in England, and the rumor is that Henry VIII composed it, but it was written several years after he died, so it's Elizabethan, not Tudor. Even so, can't you just see the king in his velvet doublet and breeches and the women in their sumptuous embroidered gowns, dancing on the green at Hampton Court?"

"Nope. But I'd forgotten your family were opera singers, honey. I'm impressed with the depth of your knowledge, but I'm going to catch you out sometime, mark my words."

They both laughed and held hands as they rounded the corner that led to the seafront walkway. The tinny notes became louder. Thatch and Tosca followed the music to its source and stopped in front of a dock where a large sport fishing boat was tied up. A ladder led up to an open fly bridge, and the rear deck was equipped with a large fish box and padded bench seating.

"Very nice," said Thatch.

"Ah, so you are beginning to appreciate classical music."

"No, I mean the boat. It's a Riviera. Built in Australia. Looks to be a forty-three footer. Luxury everywhere. Bet this boat cost close to three-quarters of a million."

The sliding glass door leading into the salon was open, and they could hear the lilting music coming from inside.

"Sounds like a piano but kind of brassy. How could anyone fit it into a boat, even one of this size?" said Thatch.

"Actually, it's a spinet. It has keys like a piano, but you can tell by its tone that the one we're hearing now is really small. It could even be a portable one, which means it's basically just a short piano keyboard in a box. They're perfect for cramped spaces like a boat."

"Last thing I'd want on a boat," said Thatch.

They sat on the seawall to listen to the pianist play the final notes of the melody in a slow, drawn-out riff. When they heard no more, the couple walked back to the house, where Thatch kissed Tosca goodnight, quoting, "'To music and the drowsy chimes.'"

"Keats' poetry sounds a lot better," she said, "than 'dug with love.' I appreciate the thought. Sleep well, *keresik*."

Twenty-Six

The following morning Tosca lowered herself gently into the vintage Austin-Healey that had been her husband's car as if into a bathtub of boiling oil, trying to avoid the part of the split leather seat that pinched her bottom if she sat on it. She started the car and drove erratically and noisily to Karma's Garden Center. I really must get something else to drive, she told herself. Aside from being such a small car I can't stand these old, dry leather seats, although I do love the drop-top. It's so California.

Before Tosca had left England everyone in London had told her that as soon as she got to the sunshine state, she must drive a convertible.

Struggling to fold down the Healey's worn canvas fabric top, torn in several places, was more than Tosca wanted to handle. J.J. never garaged the Healey without first raising its top, which meant that it had to be rolled back down each time the car was driven. Even though her friends in the UK would have no way of seeing her driving around with the top up, she felt she owed it to them to drive with it down.

"You see," she explained later to Thatch, "I can't send photos home if I'm not in a convertible. Everyone is supposed to drive one here, right?"

Thatch had chuckled. "Only tourists and surfers who need one for their boards. Otherwise we find it too hot to drive around with the top down."

Tosca parked in front of the garden center's office and went in. No one. She went outside and scanned the tables that held ceramic pots and planters, then looked across to the wood structure where hanging baskets swung in the slight breeze and farther out where the fields began. Strange way to run a business, she thought. What if a customer came in to place a huge order? I could easily help myself to a pot of flowers, too.

She saw Sam walking toward her. Of course. She'd forgotten there was a handyman.

"Hello. I wonder if you'd be so kind as to tell me if Karma is around."

"Nope. Doin' the bushes at City Hall. Can I help you?" He scratched at the bandage on his arm.

"Will she be back soon?" said Tosca.

"Cain't never tell with her," said Sam. He scratched harder at his arm. "Damn plants really got me this time. Gotta rash big as a billbug."

Tosca decided she didn't really need to know what a billbug was. Instead, she offered a few soothing words and suggested he use chamomile lotion on his arms.

"'Nah, useless stuff, that. Good for baby skin, maybe, but not for the white stuff on those plants that Karma tole me about. She said the sap bleeds out when you cut the stems or the leaves. Said they're real toxic. I nicked one by mistake when I was cutting the weeds. Them Monarch cadeepillers and ayphids we get here are supposed to be the enemies of giant milkweeds, but they don't do nothin'."

"Goodness. Maybe you should burn the plants."

"No, they're okay unless you drink that stuff." He cackled loudly. "Who'd do that? I'm betting Karma tole those people whose gardens she put 'em in all about it and said not to mix it in their fresh orange juice!"

"Why would she buy the milkweeds in the first place?" said Tosca.

"Cheap, that's why. They was a real bargain. In some countries they're considered weeds. 'Course, they have a high drought tolerance so they work well here with this bone dry weather we suffer from, damn drought."

"Yes, the drought. I sympathize more than you can possibly know. Would you mind showing me what a giant milkweed looks like?"

"Sure."

Sam led the way past several wooden tables holding plastic pots of seedlings in the gazebo area. He stopped at a small, untidy plot of land that held two shrubs. Both had whitish, cork-like stems, thick branches, leathery pale green leaves and small, five-star flowers.

"There they are," Sam said, pointing. "They bear pods with seeds inside along with silk-like fibers. These two are not for sale, and a damn good thing, too, after that there woman died, and we learned about the poisonous sap that bleeds out."

"These look like they're going to grow into trees," said Tosca.

"That's 'cause we've had them quite a while. Karma ordered these two to see if they'd be suitable for her customers, since they were such a bargain. She liked 'em, but I bet she didn't tell them people they could grow this big."

"They're kind of ugly. Are they evergreens?"

"Yep, and they need hardly any maintenance. Guess Karma liked that, too. Less work for her."

Tosca left the garden center in deep thought. It appeared as though Karma had unintentionally sold poisonous giant milkweed to her clients. Did that mean any of those six people, and Karma made it seven, could have poisoned Sally at the party? Had all of them attended that evening? And what motive could they have anyway? The answer had to be closer to Karma's inner circle, certainly anyone with a Fuller

Sanderson connection, and yet there must have been plenty of party guests who lived on Isabel Island and knew her family.

Twenty-Seven

Back on the island Tosca parked in the garage without raising the convertible top, the devil with J.J., and ran upstairs. She was anxious to start her investigation of the six homeowners and their plants before that copper beat her to the punch.

Now that she had a description of the plants, she could begin a hunt for them in the neighbors' gardens. All I have to do, she figured, is find the yards where Karma placed the giant milkweed and see if their stems have been cut.

Sam said there wasn't much sap on the ones at the garden center because Kama had sold the best ones to her customers, and the sap on the plants he touched was only enough to cause a rash on one arm, not both. Had Karma already collected enough sap to put in Sally's cocktail and murder her? Who else would want the publisher dead?

Making sure she had her iPhone with her, she began walking down the street, peering into each front yard to look for the plants Sam had shown her.

"Hi, there, Tosca, checking up on our hollyhocks?" said a woman coming out of her front door and locking it. She chuckled and added, "I don't have any, as you can see, but the weeds could use your help."

"Oh, no, Mrs. Latham, just admiring your beautiful lobelia border, one of my favorites. I was wondering if your gardener has added any giant milkweed to your flower beds, but I don't see any."

"I'm not sure exactly what has been planted," the woman replied. "I leave that up to the landscaper. Got to run, I'm off to the mall. See you later."

Tosca continued on the other side of the street, then up and down other streets, not bothering to stop at houses where the yards were paved over or those whose planters and flower beds held only cactus. At one of the houses that bordered the canal, she found a giant milkweed with a deep gash on its stem. She took a photo of it with her phone, then knocked on the door.

An old man, stooped, gaunt and dressed in a plaid shirt and khaki pants that hung loosely on his thin frame, opened the door.

"Yes?"

"Terribly sorry to bother you. I do hope you weren't taking a nap, but I wondered if you knew that your giant milkweed has been damaged."

"It has?" The man hobbled out. Tosca preceded him to the side fence where they both regarded the plant.

"Well, it doesn't look dead," the man said, "but that's a large cut. Wonder how that happened? Who'd do such a thing?"

"Your wife or grandchildren, perhaps?"

"No, ma'am, I live alone, and my grandkids are in Florida. Hmm. Nothing to be done, I suppose, until the gardener comes tomorrow."

"You mean Karma?" said Tosca.

"Yes. She'll know what to do. She sure has a green thumb."

And maybe a white one, thought Tosca.

"I took a photo of your plant, and I'd like to take a few more. Is that all right?" she asked.

"Sure, it's fine."

Tosca used her cell phone camera to take several additional pictures of the long, vertical cut on the giant milkweed stem before bidding the man goodbye and continuing on her way. After three hours of walking up and down every street on the island, she'd found five more of the plants, all with gouges to their stems. One yard contained two pots of giant milkweed. Such deadly beauty, she thought, touching the dainty purple flowers gently at the last yard she stopped at.

None of the other homeowners answered her knock or bell ring. Realizing it was the middle of the afternoon, she assumed they were at work. She took photos of all the slashed plants and wrote down the addresses. Deciding she had located all of the murderous, albeit innocent, weapons, Tosca walked to Main Street and bought a cup of strawberry ice cream topped with hot chocolate sauce. Before leaving the store she also bought a carton to take home.

Twenty-Eight

After six o'clock, when she assumed the absent homeowners would now be home, Tosca called at Arlene's house, hoping to catch her in. She took the carton of strawberry ice cream with her, knowing how much Arlene liked it.

Her friend, swathed in an outsized black and white striped butcher's apron, opened the door with kitchen mittens on her hands. An aroma of cookies baking wafted out.

"Hi, you're just in time to try my new recipe," said Arlene. Tosca handed her the carton. "Oh, no," said Arlene. "Ice cream? Wish I could have some, but the doctor says I eat too much sugar. Tom will appreciate it, though."

"Aren't those cookies you're baking full of sugar?"

"No, I'm using honey instead. It seems to have changed the consistency, though, and they've spread all over the baking sheet into one huge cookie. Come on in. I need to cut them into squares before they cool."

She stood aside to let Tosca walk by and go into the kitchen.

"Arlene, are you doing anything this evening?"

"No, not really. Tom's got his poker night next door, and I was going to watch a TV movie. Why?"

"Would you mind taking a walk with me to a few neighbors' homes here on the island?"

"Tosca, you've got that look in your eye. What's going on?"

"You've lived here a long time. I'd like you to tell me if you know the people at the houses where I took some photos today."

"Why did you do that?"

"We know Sally was poisoned by a plant with stems that ooze toxic sap. I found quite a few yards around here that have them. They're called giant milkweeds."

"Wow, are you sleuthing again? How exciting. You mean, go out after midnight and prowl around?"

Tosca laughed. "No, no, nothing as dramatic. I mean now, while it's still light, if you can."

Arlene opened a drawer, removed a knife and turned to the baking sheet. "Okay. Let me cut these apart, and we can go."

She stacked the cookie squares onto a tray, removed the apron and took a jacket from the hall coat stand as they left the house. They walked several blocks to the nearest address Tosca had written down and stood across the street from it.

"Do you know the people who live there?" said Tosca.

"No, never met them."

"Let's see if anyone's home."

There was no bell or door knocker, so they rapped on the door. The house was a one-story cottage with a small front yard of grass. Two trees supported a hammock slung between them, and beneath the front window were three stone slabs on which sat pots of flowers. A milkweed plant was among them.

The door opened to reveal a young child. She was holding a spoon, her mouth surrounded by gobs of what appeared to be blueberry ice cream.

"Hello, pet," said Tosca. "Is your mummy home?"

At that moment an elderly woman appeared behind the girl.

"Marci, go back into the kitchen." The girl turned and left, and the woman looked inquiringly at Arlene and Tosca.

"Sorry to bother you. Are you the homeowner?" said Arlene.

"I'm Marci's grandma." She crossed her arms. "There's a sign right there on the window that says 'No Soliciting.'"

"No, no. I'm one of your neighbors, Arlene Mindel. I live down the street, and this is Tosca Trevant, visiting from London. We're not selling anything. We just want to ask about those two big plants over there."

"What about them?"

"Did you see who might have cut the stems?"

The woman walked over to the pots and peered at the slashes.

"Well, upon my soul. Students again, I suppose. They're always playing around in the hammock. I don't know why Patty leaves it out here. Maybe they cut the stems of these plants for what they think is fun."

"So you don't know who may have damaged them?" said Tosca.

"No, sorry, no idea."

Tosca thanked the woman, and she and Arlene left, deciding there was no further information coming from the household.

"How about here?" said Tosca, indicating the next address on her list. In the front yard a giant milkweed was planted in a waist-high clay pot.

"Yes, this is Cynthia and George Stanowski's house. They've lived here for many years. They're an elderly couple with no children. Do you want to meet them?"

At Tosca's nod, Arlene rang the front doorbell. A large woman with short, white hair opened the door and peered at the visitors.

"Oh, it's you, Arlene, didn't recognize you at first." Her voice was scratchy but soft. "Would you like to come in? Excuse the mess. We just got back an hour ago from staying with friends in Carmel."

"Thank you, Cynthia. This is my friend, Tosca. She's staying with her daughter here on the island."

Tosca closed the screen door behind her as they entered straight into a living room. The television was on, and a man whom Tosca assumed was George sat in a recliner, his feet on the raised footrest.

"Don't get up," Arlene said quickly. "We can't stay long, but Tosca has a question or two, if you don't mind."

George picked up the remote from a side table and turned the television sound off, looking at the visitors curiously.

"Questions?"

"Yes," said Tosca, "about the new plant in your garden, the giant milkweed."

"Oh? Karma brought it over a couple of weeks ago. She does our landscaping, such as it is. Nice flowers, aren't they? We'd never seen one before. She told us it was from India. Why?"

"Have you noticed that the stem has a gash in it?"

"No, we've been away. I haven't taken a good look at the yard yet since we got back."

"Then you must have missed Karma's party last week.'

"Yes, we were sorry we couldn't attend, but we're going to donate to the Sanderson library. Sounds like a worthwhile project. My parents were friends with Fuller and Abigail, but after they died we didn't keep in touch with his son, nor with Destiny."

"Wasn't it sad about that woman's death at the party?" said Cynthia. "My neighbor told me about it when we called in to see if everything was all right at our house. She's been keeping an eye on it for us. Was it a stroke?"

"No," said Arlene. "We're told she was poisoned."

George swung his legs off the footrest, and Cynthia put her hand over her mouth.

"Poisoned? That's shocking," said her husband.

"Yes," said Tosca, "with giant milkweed sap. That's why we're here asking about your plant."

Twenty-Nine

George and Cynthia both spoke at once, assuring Tosca and Arlene that they had been away and knew nothing about poisonous sap.

Deciding the visit was another dead end, Tosca and Arlene thanked the couple, took their leave and continued on to the third address.

"Ah, this is where Sunny lives," said Arlene. "She's a librarian at the Newport Beach library, and she belongs to our bunco group. Let's see if she's in."

A small cottage set between two others of the same size, its small front yard was filled with dozens of small and large pots. The women entered through the small gate and inspected the pots.

"There's the one with the cut stem," Tosca said, pointing to a tall terra cotta jar.

No bell or door knocker was in sight, but the front door was open behind the screen door. Arlene called out, "Sunny, are you home? It's Arlene."

A short young woman appeared, holding a kitten against her shoulder.

"Arlene! How nice to see you. Let me unlatch the screen door. Come on in."

Tosca was introduced, and she quickly gave the reason for their visit, explaining about milkweed plants and their toxicity to both humans and animals. She told Sunny that the stem on the plant in the large jar outside her front door had been slit.

"Slit? How strange. Let's go out, and you can show me."

The three went outside, and Tosca pointed out the damage.

"I've never noticed it,' said Sunny. "When do you think it happened?"

"Maybe a week or so ago," said Tosca. "It looks quite fresh, just like the cuts to the other ones we've seen on the island. They are all recent plantings."

"Do you think Karma may have done it by mistake, at least in mine, when she was putting it in? I'm usually at work when she comes here."

"You weren't at her party, Sunny, were you? I didn't see you there," said Arlene.

"No, Karma invited me but I was in San Diego, visiting my sister."

Tosca and Arlene took their leave, noting they only had two more houses to check out and hoping their owners were in.

Five streets over, facing the bay and the peninsula, with a sweeping view of the harbor, they stopped at a three-story stone mansion on a double lot. It towered above its neighbors, which were equally as palatial but not as tall or imposing. The front yard included two tiered rock gardens in opposite corners, a large grass area and three planters, one of which held an exceptionally bushy milkweed.

"Oh, yes," said Arlene, looking up at the copper-topped cupola on the roof. "This is where Betty and Sol Bernstein live. A nice couple. They built this house a couple of years ago. She's a big donor to the arts. Didn't you meet them at Karma's party? They were both there."

"No. Sally became ill before I had the chance to talk to everyone. Let's see if they're home. Oh, look. Wave, Arlene. We're on *Candid Camera*." Tosca pointed to the four small black security cameras positioned above the doorway.

While Arlene reached up to the shiny brass lion-head that served as a knocker on the front door and banged it twice, Tosca went over to examine the plant she knew so well by now. Careful not to touch the large vertical cut in its thick stem, she reflected that the killer might have gathered enough of the poison from just this one plant.

Could it be that the others had been slashed to draw suspicion away from the Bernstein's milkweed?

A woman's disembodied voice came through a small box on one side of the doorframe.

"Yes?"

"Hi, Betty, it's Arlene. I'd forgotten you have a security system. Can we talk to you for a moment?"

"Oh, of course, dear. What a nice surprise. Just a second, I'll be right there."

The tall door was pulled back, and a woman appeared. Her tightly coiffed, stiff hairdo and full-length blue jacquard gown gave Tosca the impression of a duchess awaiting friends for tea. Betty invited her visitors in.

Tosca was introduced, and she and Arlene were led into a library. Floor to ceiling cherry wood bookshelves lined the walls with volumes of books interspersed with knickknacks. A baby grand piano occupied one corner, a music stand to its right.

"Wasn't Karma's party fun, that is, until Sally became ill?" said Betty. "I had just mentioned to you, Arlene, that she seemed to be drunk, but now we know she was sick. I can't believe she died."

"Yes, it was very sad. Tosca was at the party, too, and wants to ask you something."

"Really?" Betty turned to Tosca, her eyebrows raised. "How can I help you?"

"I know it's a bit of a cheek asking you this, but I wondered if you or your husband had any dealings, business or otherwise, with Sally and her publishing house. I seem to remember that you told me Sol collects first editions."

"Good heavens, yes, that's right. He's in Japan at the moment, chasing down some rare book, and he's always asking Sally if she knows of any serious book collectors who have Fuller first editions. She always says no, but Sol suspects she must have the entire collection, knowing the longer Sally keeps them, the more they'll be worth. Let me show you his collection; he's real proud of it."

She led them through the hall and into a study where a tall, glass-fronted cabinet stretched from one side of a wall to the other. On the shelves were hundreds of hardcover books, most leather bound, with several of the titles in gilt. A few paperbacks were evident in pristine condition.

"Sol heard a rumor that Sally might close up shop because she was broke," said Betty, "and we were willing to pay a hefty sum for the first editions." She turned to Arlene. "You seem to know so much about the Sandersons. Have you heard anything about the estate and its contents? She must have left a will. I wonder who's the beneficiary? I bet she owned all of Sanderson's first editions. I know Sol would do anything to get his hands on them."

Tosca was taken aback by the callousness of the reply and was momentarily thrown off course.

Arlene answered, "Betty, we know that Sally was in financial difficulty, but I have no idea about a will."

"My husband is obsessed with buying a first edition of *The Total Surrender*. Have you read any of Sanderson's books, Tosca?"

Tempted to reply that she owned every single one of Sanderson's first editions just to see Betty's reaction, Tosca instead changed the subject.

"You do know that Sally was poisoned? And that it was with the sap from giant milkweed plants? You have two pots of them in your front garden. I noticed that the stems have been cut. Traces of the sap are still there where it's been collected. It was put in the White Russians she drank."

Betty gaped at Tosca and straightened up in her chair. "Good heavens, you don't think either Sol or I know what's in our yard, do you? Karma comes in every week and takes care of it. We have no idea what the plants are or what they're called."

Arlene stood up, clearly upset. "Of course you don't, dear. We're just trying to figure something out, that's all. Tosca gets a little carried away sometimes. She's English, you know."

"Cornish." Tosca spluttered the word as she, too, stood up and held out her hand. "Thank you for a fascinating conversation. Much food for thought. By the way, with such a valuable collection in the house, you are smart to have installed security cameras outside. I wonder if we might take a look at the tapes?"

"The tapes? Sol takes care of all that."

"Perhaps we can have your permission to view them at your security company offices?"

"I'm sorry, you'll have to ask my husband when he returns."

Thirty

On the way to the next house Tosca asked Arlene her opinion. Was Sol the kind of person who would kill in order to satisfy his obsession with first editions?

"Oh, Tosca, I can't imagine that Sol would kill anyone. That's absurd. Although, now that you ask, I read true crime books, and sometimes it's the nice guy next door who turns out to be a murderer. So I have to say I'm not sure. I don't know him that well, but he and Betty seem like a very ordinary couple."

"It's a little far-fetched, I suppose," said Tosca. "I wonder if Sol knew for sure that Sally had first editions. If she was so broke, she probably sold them all off, but it was interesting how Betty missed the whole point of my question. She sidestepped by saying she didn't know anything about her plants instead of answering whether she noticed they'd been cut."

The next-to-last address on Tosca's list was a dilapidated duplex, but the garden looked well taken care of. Probably Karma's work, noted Arlene, telling Tosca that she knew neither the current tenants nor the homeowner. Her opinion that Karma was the gardener was confirmed when Tosca pointed out the signature milkweed planted in a circle of soil in the center. Tosca quickly checked the stem and was surprised to see a very small cut, only a third of the size of the other slashes.

A For Rent sign was in the downstairs window. There were no drapes, and when they looked through the glass, the rooms were empty. They went to the back of the house and found a flight of wooden steps that led upstairs. On the door was another For Rent sign.

"Maybe it's a tear-down," said Arlene. "Looks in pretty bad condition. The paint's peeling all over the place. Guess they've all moved out. Didn't you see the For Rent signs when you came by earlier?"

"Yes, I did see them, but I was hoping the owner might be around now, hoping to catch possible renters' attention, and be here to answer questions. Neither of the signs have any contact phone numbers."

"So let's move on to the final house," said Arlene.

Tosca was silent as they walked seven more blocks, deciding that the killer had most likely collected enough sap at the other houses to leave the plant at the empty houses barely touched. She also wondered what had been used to collect the poison. A glass jar? What would I use? The lab report said only a small amount could cause death. I think I'd use something I had around the house, or I'd buy a small jar of baby food at the supermarket, clean it out, and put the sap in. No, that would be too big to bring to the party and too noticeable. It could be carried in a woman's purse, she conceded to herself, but not in a man's pocket. So perhaps the murderer was one of the female party guests.

In addition, how would the killer manage to empty the sap surreptitiously, whatever it was contained in, into Sally's drink with so many people crowded around the bar, if that's where it happened? Of course. She remembered Blair had given up his place in line until he was the last one, giving him privacy to add the poison, she believed, to the cocktail.

At the final house the two women entered the yard through a rusty iron gate. Tosca scanned the area quickly and spotted the milkweed. It was near the low stucco wall that separated it from the neighbor's yard.

"It looks fine from here," said Arlene, peering over at the plant's stem. "I don't see any cuts."

"My photo shows otherwise."

She walked to the wall and bent down.

"Yes. There's a cut just like all the others."

At the homeowner's door Arlene rang the bell, setting off furious barking from inside, the same barking that Tosca had heard when she visited the house earlier in the day. There had been no response then, but she'd lingered long enough to admire the door's two mullioned glass panels and the carved wood Tudor rose in the door's center.

"I think the architect has mixed Tudor with Elizabethan, but it's still beautiful," said Tosca to Arlene, reaching up to run her fingers over the red, green and white rose.

"Really? I think it's a gorgeous door. Tosca, sometimes you are a little too critical. You should be pleased to see a reminder of old England over here, no offense."

"The deliberate substitution and switching around of our historical eras can be jarring to the eyes of a foreigner like me, I suppose. Oh, the dog has stopped barking."

The door was opened by a young Asian man holding a German shepherd by its collar.

"Yes?"

"Sorry to bother you," said Tosca. "We were admiring your Japanese garden and plantings, especially the miniature red bridge over that little river of stones. Charming."

The three looked over at the garden feature that took up most of the front yard.

"Thank you," he said

Arlene held out her hand toward him. "We're neighbors. Arlene Mindel, and this is Tosca Trevant."

"Harry Tanaka. What can I do for you?"

He shook their hands. Tosca was surprised that his accent was pure American and surmised he was born and raised in the United States.

"We were wondering about the plant at the far end of the bridge," she said, "the giant milkweed with the tiny purple flowers. The stem is broken, or rather, it seems to have a deep gash in it. Had you noticed?"

The three walked toward the plant and inspected the stem. Tosca pointed out the damaged stem.

"No," said Tanaka, "I haven't noticed anything. Maybe a cat took a dislike to it." He chuckled. "Is that why you stopped by?"

He bent down to touch the tiny drop of sap that remained on the stem.

"No, don't touch it!" said Tosca. "It can cause a rash!"

Tanaka jumped back at her vehement outburst and looked at her in consternation.

"I'm sorry," said Arlene. "We needed to warn you. Is Karma your gardener?"

"Yes, she is, but my landlady takes care of the maintenance. I've only rented here for a year. The yard was a mess when I arrived, and then I had the idea for the little bridge. Reminds me of Japanese gardens. Karma asked the owner if she could build it for me and was given permission to do so."

"We've seen that same kind of plant in five other yards, and all of them have had their stems slashed," said Tosca, bringing his attention back to the milkweed. "Have you ever heard of Karma's grandfather, Fuller Sanderson, the author?"

"I know hardly anyone on Isabel Island. I've only seen Karma a couple of times. I'm studying math at UCI and don't have much time for reading anything but text books. Who is Fuller Sanderson?"

After explaining that the illustrious former island resident was long gone, Tosca asked Tanaka if he knew of the party at Kama's house at which a guest had died.

"No," he said. "I don't even read the newspapers. My finals are coming up."

His visitors left and headed home.

"Another one we can rule out," said Tosca. "Thanks for your help, Arlene. I think I'll sleep well tonight having satisfied my curiosity about the milkweeds in all those yards."

"You sure look pretty smug," said Arlene.

"Do I?"

"I thought it seemed to be a bust. Were any of those people a help?"

"Yes, but I can't tell you why at the moment."

She didn't want to explain to Arlene how pleased she was that they'd been able to talk to the homeowners before that surly police detective interviewed them, nor did she want her friend to know exactly how her own inquiries were proceeding. She liked Arlene very much but knew of her inclination to gossip.

Takes one to know one, Tosca admitted wryly to herself.

After they parted company at Arlene's house and went their separate ways. Tosca went home to get the car and drove over to the Newport Beach police station located on the perimeter of the city's famous fashion plaza. She asked to speak with Parnell.

"I have some photographs to show you," she said when he appeared.

"What photographs?"

"Of the damaged stems on the giant milkweed plants, where the murderer got the sap."

"You were trespassing again?"

"Oh, no. My neighbor and I were invited in by each homeowner except at the house with no tenants. One of the homes has security cameras. Maybe the murderer is shown on tape colleting some sap. Wouldn't you like to check it out?"

The detective took Tosca's phone to have the photos printed out and made a note of all the homeowners' addresses. After half an hour Parnell returned and gave the phone back to Tosca. He led her out and bade her a curt goodnight.

Thirty-One

"How many Alzheimer patients did you and Christine get to listen to with that music program yesterday?" asked Tosca as she and J.J. had coffee and homemade scones on the roof patio the next morning. From their vantage point they had a clear view of one of the two canals that encircled the island, and they looked up whenever a yacht sailed slowly by.

"We managed to work with seven of them," said J.J., "three men and four women who were willing to try out the iPods and headphones we brought. We had a difficult time at first because we asked them what music they liked, but most didn't remember. They just looked at us blankly. So we picked out what we decided was from their high school years, after we learned their approximate ages from the nurse, and most of them really perked up."

"What a splendid idea. Music & Memory, Inc. Is that the name? Must have been heartwarming."

"Yes. The medical staff were amazed to see their patients reawaken. One old fella hadn't spoken in three years, nor smiled, and there he was, grinning from ear to ear, when we put the headphones on him. He kept saying, 'Yeah, yeah.' It was such fun to see most of the patients respond, keeping time with the music by nodding their heads. One woman started to do a jig. We played some Irish folk songs for her, and she began to talk about Dublin, said it was her hometown."

"Tell me more. I'm so pleased you have this interest in music, even if it isn't opera."

"That's where you're wrong, Mummy. One woman had been a cellist with a Utah symphony orchestra, according to her medical file. We played part of an aria from *La Boheme*, and she began to talk about the opera. The nurse said she hadn't uttered a word in months."

Tosca wanted more details about the program. J.J. showed her a brochure that explained how musical memory is linked to emotions and that memories are stored deep within the brain. While Alzheimer's damages the ability to recall facts and details, it does not destroy the lasting connections between a favorite song and memory of an important life event that was associated with it, no matter how long ago.

Tosca wondered aloud which musical memories would reawaken her if she suffered from Alzheimer's.

"Any and all operas for you," said J.J. "Mine would be the whine of an Indy car engine."

As if on cue, both were distracted by a deep rapping noise that caused them to watch a speedboat race by, setting the calm waters splashing over the sides of the low sea wall.

"Hear that rod knock from the boat's engine?" said J.J. "Those bearings won't last long."

"Yes, dear, I'm sure you're right. But look how the water came up over the wall. Does it ever flood here?"

"It did once many years ago, I was told. I've never seen water come onto the walkway except when boats like that one ignore the rules. If they keep it up, the harbormaster will be after them. I should take you over to the Wedge if you want to see crashing waves. It's a famous surfing spot with huge breaks that slam into the beach after bouncing off the jetty there. Only the most daredevil of bodysurfers and foolish tourists swim the Wedge when the waves are gigantic. They're like a wall of water, a tsunami. Every year someone breaks his neck or gets seriously injured and ends up paraplegic after they get slammed in the riptide."

"Why aren't people warned off?"

"They are. There's a large red sign cautioning against diving or jumping off the jetty and warning people about the submerged, slippery rocks and strong currents. High surf advisories are announced over the radio, too, when the waves are considered dangerous."

Tosca shuddered. "Sounds like a death trap."

"It can be. There's a strong undertow that drags people back into the surf when they're trying to get out of the water and onto the beach."

"Is it like that year round?"

J.J. said, "No, but this is the time of the year for a tropical depression or a storm, and the effect on the Wedge can bring waves thirty feet or higher. It's a favorite pastime of the locals to stand and watch, and if they come too close to the surf, they can be dragged in by the riptide."

"I'll stick with being a landlubber, thank you, even though your grandfather was a champion water polo player. He taught me to swim in the Celtic Sea area of the Atlantic Ocean. It was pretty rough with huge waves. I never really enjoyed it."

Tosca took their breakfast dishes to the sink, rinsed them off and loaded them into the dishwasher.

"Guess that's a hint for me to finish clearing the table so you can set up your laptop," said J.J., putting the condiments on the kitchen counter and sliding the red placemats into a drawer. "I have practice today at the Long Beach track, followed by a birthday party for one of the crew, so I won't see you till tonight."

She went off to get showered and dressed, returned within twenty minutes and grabbed her NASCAR racing helmet on her way out the door.

That helmet looks like it weighs a ton, reflected Tosca. It's a wonder it doesn't break her neck. *Rem' fey*, I wish she'd chosen a different career than auto racing. Too much like her Dad, rest his soul

Thirty-Two

On his boat Blair closed the lid of the sixteenth century ottovino spinet he'd been playing, snapped its rusty clasp closed and slid the instrument into a black canvas carrying case. It was his favorite of the several rare instruments he'd collected over his lifetime, probably because the two-foot-long triangle-shaped mahogany spinet with its Swiss pine soundboard had been the most difficult to acquire. It was built by craftsmen in Toledo, Spain, and although Blair had no idea how it came to be in America, he considered it a lucky find. On the inside of the lid was a faded, hand-painted seascape of a three-masted tall ship etched in gold, its rigging almost devoid of color.

When he'd heard the instrument's odd, tinny tones coming from the basement floor of a dilapidated New York apartment building next to where he lived, he'd stood transfixed. He was fifteen years old and had a passion to play music since he was seven. His father, Taylor "Tinky" Blair, was a literary agent whose major client was Fuller Sanderson, at the height of his fame as an author. Tinky refused to let his boy take lessons, planning his son's future as a lawyer.

When he was nine years old, Blair had stolen a guitar from his school band's closet and taught himself to play without knowing how to read sheet music. He had the gift of playing by ear. After listening to a tune he could copy it almost instantly. He secreted the guitar in the basement of one of Manhattan's lower East Side's abandoned buildings and spent most of his free hours after school over the next few years hanging around music stores on Seventh Avenue. A few years later he became friends with some old-timers, most of them retired musicians who sat on battered chairs on the sidewalk outside the music stores. The men were pleased with the attention and happy to talk to the talented teen. Blair would bring his guitar and pluck the strings, enjoying comments from admirers and learning as much as he could.

At eighteen he got a job in a music store, much to his father's chagrin. They soon parted ways. After a while Graydon tired of the contemporary rock, rap, hip-hop, and techno-pop that blared through the store's loudspeakers all day and half the night. His heart lay in the classics, and he'd sneak into the tradesmen's doors at concert venues, at times hidden in a vendor truck or dressed as a delivery boy, to gain entry into Carnegie Hall and the Metropolitan Opera House. He'd find a hiding spot and listen, entranced. Even when locked, the doors had been relatively easy to open for a young man used to breaking and entering to steal the musical instruments he coveted.

Blair Sr. relocated to California to be nearer his famous client, author Fuller Sanderson. In an effort to reunite with his son, Blair Sr. invited him to join him but was refused. Not until his father died six years later did Graydon visit the West Coast and realize how lucrative the agency was, thanks to its famous client.

After burying Tinky Blair, the young Blair took over the business and for the next several years enjoyed his large percentage of profits from the Sanderson book royalties. The money allowed him to maintain his father's house on Isabel Island and buy the Riviera boat, even traveling to Australia to meet the boat builder and designer; but eventually Sanderson's books became less and less popular, and Blair's income dwindled to almost nothing.

With second mortgages already on his house and the Riviera, he knew that his dire financial straits would soon force him to surrender both to the banks for foreclosure unless his new plan was successful.

The most precious and highly valuable possessions he owned were the five rare musical instruments that formed his collection. He vowed they would never be sold. He prized the elongated, pear-shaped, fifteenth century rebec; the guitar-like eighteenth century chitarra battente; and the rectangular, thirteenth century, harp-like Welsh crwth. He took great pride, too, in owning the medieval Italian ottavino spinet with its magnificent hand-painted illustration on the inside of the lid. Then there was his ancient Israelite harp whose strings, he knew, should be plucked very gently. In modern Hebrew the instrument was referred to as a Kinnor harp, placing it in the category of Western violins, and Blair often used the name to clarify its origin.

He lavished tenderness on the instruments, stroking their fine old wood when he wasn't playing them and obsessively checking the strings and parts. Blair was talented enough to play all five and could have joined a regional orchestra or played informally with a local group, but he knew if he brought any of his treasures along with him to perform, should such an opportunity arise, it would trigger too much comment. No, he'd gone to plenty of trouble to build the collection, and besides, he didn't want anyone else asking to play or even touch any of them.

The theremin was a different case. He'd bought it himself, and he considered it no great possession. The earliest instruments dated back only to the 1920s, much too recent to have any significance for a serious collector, Blair believed. Nevertheless, what had caught his interest in owning a theremin was its uniqueness, its application as a musical instrument that had evolved from the research of a Russian physicist, Leon Theremin.

Testing proximity sensors, the scientist was startled to hear the electronic instrument emit strange sounds when he moved his hands in the vicinity of its two antennae without actually coming into physical contact with them. Musicians were drawn to the theremin's potential, and it became part of concert symphony orchestras and pop bands and morphed into the Moog synthesizer.

High on Blair's list of favorites was the small spinet he had just been playing. Barely two feet long, it nevertheless overlapped the boat's galley table because of its triangular shape. Blair was forced to stand up or sit on a high stool to play it. An alternative he'd considered was to acquire an even smaller one, but he decided he didn't really need it. To his knowledge, which was extensive as far as collectors of ancient musical instruments went, there was no one who owned an ottavino spinet that was earlier than the seventeenth century. He'd looked into spinet kits, thinking to build his own just for kicks, but his excitement came from old, rare instruments and the thrill of ownership. Knowing he had wrested his away from its rightful owner added to his satisfaction.

Loud laughter and the sound of tinkling glasses from the large yacht at the adjoining slip interrupted his reminiscences. He turned around to the bar in his galley, poured a generous half-glass of bourbon and went onto the deck. To the west the setting sun was a soft orange, almost hidden as it prepared to sink below the horizon. He looked at his watch and realized it was way past the cocktail hour.

Blair climbed the cherry-wood ladder to the flybridge and flung himself into the captain's chair, almost spilling his drink. Thank God that stupid moron Sally was gone, he thought. There would probably be turmoil at her floundering publishing house for a while, but eventually it would be closed down. Sally had neglected the business as she aged and had been on the brink of bankruptcy for months, maybe years. Only her secretary remained at the office.

Now, at last, Blair had the opportunity he'd been seeking to take Sanderson's works to another publisher and earn a lot of money. Sally had never bothered to make an audio book recording of the titles or even allow e-books to be formatted and sold. Once Karma signed a new contract, giving him control, he could mine those outlets alone for tens of thousands of dollars. Reissuing all of the books individually, as well as packaging them into three-volume printings and designing new, more up-to-date covers, presented even more potential.

There was still Swenson to deal with, but Blair knew he could easily be bought off or intimidated. The Tubby Ghost, he called him, although the man was far from a wisp. Strange, Blair always thought Scandinavians, even those born in the U.S., would be tall and skinny. He had to admit, though, that Swenson sure could write up a storm.

The noise from the neighboring boat increased as six people appeared from the stateroom, chatting and holding drinks. Two of them waved to Blair, who hoisted his own glass in salute.

"Come on over," said a young man, approaching the rail nearest Blair. Like the others, he wore swimwear. He had an arm around a leggy brunette whose red bikini barely covered her generous curves.

"Thanks, Joel, not today."

"Aw, come on, Gray. Bring one of those weird guitars of yours. My Dad's tired of listening to my hip-hop."

"Thanks again, but I'm celebrating something elsewhere." He forced a smile. Blair disliked being called Gray, and he had a feeling Joel knew it.

"Hey, we've got plenty of champagne. Celebrating what?"

Blair shook his head and didn't answer. He climbed down, holding his drink, and entered the cabin. He rinsed out his glass, picked up the spinet in its carrying case and slid the wide strap over his shoulder. Then he stepped onto the dock and headed for his A-frame house four blocks away.

With the plan already in place, he assured himself he'd be solvent and safe within weeks. Maybe he'd better go to the bank and explain the new circumstances so that his house and boat would not suffer foreclosure.

He also hoped that the others realized Sally's demise was most fortuitous for all concerned.

Thirty-Three

Tosca bade Thatch goodnight and climbed the steps to J.J.'s apartment to find her daughter listening to music.

"That's an old one, must be the mid-1990s, isn't it?"

"Yes," said J.J. "Abba. Don't you remember I almost wore their CDs out when I was twelve?"

"I do indeed. You wore me out, too. Are you having a nostalgic moment?"

"No. Yes. It has to do with the visit to the Alzheimer's patients' homes I went to with Christine while you were off with her dad doing your thing in San Diego. I told you that there's been a breakthrough using music to reawaken memories, didn't I?"

"Vaguely. Sorry, love, but there's been a lot going on these days. Tell me more."

J.J. explained that current research by neuroscientists had proven that when some Alzheimer patients listened to their favorite music from the past, their brains responded by remembering the lyrics and even the circumstances of the time.

"It can help those with dementia reconnect to the world, unlocking their emotions. Some of the patients who have not spoken in years begin singing the words, regaining the ability to talk once again."

"I know music is a universal language," said Tosca, "but this sounds amazing."

"It is. I did some research about music and the brain and found a book called *Musicophilia* that says response to music is preserved, even if dementia is very advanced, stimulating cognitive powers, among others, because musical perception, sensitivity, emotion and memory can survive long after other forms of memory have disappeared. The author, Oliver Sacks, points out that music is not just auditory and emotional but motoric as well."

"Motoric?" said Tosca. "Is that one of your racing terms? It's certainly not a musical one."

J.J. laughed and shook her head. "Wrong, Mummy. It boils down to the notion that we listen to music with our muscles as well as our ears and brain. Most people involuntarily start tapping, moving their feet or their whole body when they hear rhythm. The Alzheimer's patients did exactly that."

J.J. explained that Oliver Sacks, a physician and the author who also wrote the book *Awakenings,* later made into a movie, discovered music has a powerful effect on the brain, which was proved when she and Christine talked to the patients at the homes.

"Must have been a heartwarming experience," said Tosca. "I've often wondered if music, the language of the universe, should be blared out into space to look for aliens like it was in that movie, *Close Encounters of the Third Kind.* Remember the five-tone scale the pianist kept playing to communicate with the spaceship?"

"Come back to earth, Mother, I want to tell you more about this program. One problem is funding. The patients need iPods or some other digital audio device to listen to the music with. One of the saddest parts of our visit today was to learn from the social workers that many of the people at the home are poor. It's a state facility, and, of course, they never have enough money. No way can they afford to supply iPods, so I'm going to organize a fundraiser for them."

"Admirable, dear. Perhaps you can donate a portion of your next race winnings."

"Already arranged, Mum."

"How about asking teens to donate their iPods? I assume they can be wiped clean? Be a blessing in disguise. Must be thousands of mothers who'd thank you."

"That'd be like condemning the kids to prison," said J.J. "There have been crimes committed for less. Well, I'm off to bed. Goodnight, Mother."

Her daughter's last words about crimes brought Tosca's thoughts back to Sally's sudden death. It was now common knowledge that she'd been poisoned. *I suppose that Parnell chappie is in charge of the investigation*, she mused. *He needs my help.*

Thirty-Four

"You still don't have the flash drive?"

Karma and Blair were at her house, drinking coffee after she returned from the hospital. Unkempt as ever, the living room was dark. Only a few shards of sunlight pierced the half-closed shutters

"No, I told you already. Oh, by the way, I'm keeping this," said Karma, picking up the locket that had fallen from Sally's purse and twirling the pendant around by its long, silver chain.

"It must be Grandmother Abigail's, although I never saw her wear it. Not really my style. The chain's too thin, and the locket's real small, but I suppose it has some value, if I decide to sell it.

"Karma, please focus. Where is the flash drive, if you don't have it? If Swenson bails on us or gets hit by a truck, we won't have anything!"

Karma slipped the locket chain over her head. "I bet Fuller gave this to Sally as a gift after grandma died," she said. "Sally shouldn't have accepted it. It's a family heirloom. I'll take it to the police today, but I want it back. I guess they'll know what to do with all her other stuff. Oh, yes, the flash drive. Are you sure Sally had it?"

Blair told her he'd been at the publishing house two weeks earlier when Swenson had come in and handed the drive to her. Sally had asked him if it was the only copy, and Swenson had assured her it was. Then Blair said he watched Sally open a desk drawer, drop the small black device in and lock the drawer. She'd thanked Swenson for bringing it along, and he left.

"I went back there again after Sally died," said Blair, "and asked Nancy, that secretary of hers, where it was. She said she had no idea. I asked her to check the locked drawer, but she refused. I went to Sally's desk myself and opened all the drawers. None of them were locked. Sally must have taken the flash drive out. Maybe it's at her house."

"I don't even know where she lives," said Karma, "but I'm sure we can find out. Perhaps you can pay a visit."

Blair allowed a small smile then said, "Oh, I forgot. Nancy wants to know about Sally's funeral. Are you arranging it?"

"Why should I"

"But surely you'll provide all the flowers from your garden center, won't you?" His silky tone annoyed Karma, but she refused to rise to the bait.

"Of course I will, Graydon," she said. "I'll be accepting donations, too. How much would you like to contribute?" Satisfied to see him taken aback, she added, "You can give me a check later when the final arrangements have been made."

Karma got up from the sofa and stood in front of him, arms akimbo. "So where do we stand?"

"No need to get hostile. Everything's fine. We just need to figure out where Sally hid the damn thing."

"Well, so what?" Karma sat down again and stretched out her legs. It doesn't matter much now, does it?"

"It'll matter plenty if anyone finds it. Did you search her car?"

"I didn't have time."

"What do you mean?" Blair was visibly upset at the news. "You have the keys, don't you? Maybe the flash drive is in her car."

"It's too late to look in it now. The car's gone. The Public Administrator's office sent someone down to take possession. I gave them the keys, and they drove it away. Seems that's standard procedure under the circumstances. Then, if no relatives show up to claim their property, it's sold at auction. You could go and bid on it," she said with a sly expression on her face. "No, I'm sure Sally would have kept the drive with her in this bag, but it isn't here."

"How well did you search?" He got up and began looking under the sofa, the desk and the two wingback chairs.

"When I got back from going with Sally to the hospital, there was a note from Arlene and that Brit woman, saying they'd cleaned up. I'm sure they left everything they found on the desk here, but maybe they didn't. I have no idea exactly what Sally had in her purse."

Thirty-Five

Tosca practically rubbed her hands together in anticipation as she changed from shorts and a T-shirt into jeans and a cropped blue top that skimmed her waist, prepared to have lunch with Thatch and find out what he had learned about the mysterious Sunida. *He'd better have as much interesting news about that person as I have about Sanderson's unpublished manuscripts,* she mused.

Aside from having found out what the flash drive revealed, she was convinced that the Chandelier that had rolled out of the publisher's purse was part of the mystery, although she could see no connection between the Sanderson manuscripts and the silver plaque on the gemstone. Certainly Thatch was astonished when he saw it. Was it Sally's? But then, who or what is Sunida?

"Maybe it belongs to one of her other authors," surmised Thatch in answer to her question when he called her earlier in the morning.

"Not according to that literary agent," Tosca said. "At the party he indicated that Hirsch House was on its uppers, almost bankrupt, in fact, and that the Sanderson books were all they had left. We can hash it out at lunch. Oops, didn't mean to make a pun, but corned beef hash sounds good."

"We'll go to The Brig in Dana Point harbor, then. See you at noon. Bring the Chandelier."

Tosca was adding a bright pink lipstick to her lips when her cell phone sounded.

"Hi, Arlene," she said. "Nice to hear your voice. I'm just about to meet Thatch for lunch. Anything important?"

"Oh, yes, indeed. Remember we all thought Sally would be cremated after the police got through their investigation of her murder and released the body, even though her killer hasn't been identified? Well, they are releasing it today, and she's going to be cremated later this week."

"Did someone claim her?"

"Karma set up a web site for donations, and several people who were guests at the party stepped forward to cover the cost."

"That's very generous. Such a shame she had no family. You do know that when bodies are cremated, their ashes are, more often than not, mixed in with ashes left over in the oven from the previous cremation."

"Tosca, you are getting ghoulish again."

"On the contrary. Now at least she'll have a friend—or part of one. I've never understood why people sprinkle a few ashes here, a few over there. What is that, an arm here, an ear there? Gosh, look at the time. Sorry, Arlene, I've got to run. Ta-ta."

After Thatch picked Tosca up for lunch, during which she indulged in crisply fried corned beef hash and poached eggs, they drove up Jamboree Boulevard and turned right onto Pacific Coast Highway. Passing the Fashion Island complex, Tosca declared, "I find it the poshest shopping available in Newport Beach, but it's not quite London's New Bond Street, is it?"

She waited for Thatch to reply. When he didn't, she asked where they were going.

"I have a surprise for you," he said.

They drove south toward Laguna Beach, past the luxury estates and gated communities built on the hills with magnificent views of the ocean. One famous author lived in a palatial estate there, as did one of America's best-loved late-night comedians and a few pro athletes, but most of their neighboring multimillionaires kept a low profile,

"You said you'd tell me how you found that Sunida person," said Tosca, "or are we going back to the mine to talk to your friend? I guess we won't be digging there again, because I don't see any equipment."

She readjusted the seatbelt and smoothed down her cotton top. "I never know how to dress when you are so mysterious."

"You look perfect, honey."

Thatch turned left off Route 1 in Laguna Beach and drove slowly down a narrow side street. An artist's colony originally attracting *plein air* painters because of its scenic beauty, the town was now a bustling tourist destination for its beaches and coves. With an international reputation, it was home to several arts festivals in which artists from all over the world exhibited. Celebrities, including Lauren Bacall and Humphrey Bogart, had discovered its charm in the 1930s, as had writer John Steinbeck.

"What's the Pageant of the Masters I just saw advertised on a banner?" said Tosca as they came into the small town.

"It an annual show, a huge attraction. More than ninety minutes of *tableaux vivants*, faithful recreations of art masterpieces and contemporary works with real people posing to look exactly like their counterparts in the original pieces. They pose without moving, like statues, for several minutes. I don't know how they do it, and it's mostly volunteer residents. I'll take you one evening. It's on till the end of August this year."

"I think that's the most you have ever said to me at any one time."

Thatch grinned and turned left again onto a small back street. He asked Tosca to look for house number 261. When she said it was the pale tan bungalow on the right, he stopped and angled his truck between two motorcycles, improvising a parking spot. "Who lives here?" she asked.

"Sunida."

The tiny front yard was unkempt, and the walkway to the front door was missing a few paving stones. The faded, stained stucco and roof tiles presented a general air of neglect, prompting Tosca to whisper, "If that Chandelier's worth what you say it is, why on earth would Sunida, and you haven't said whether it's male or female, live in this old place?"

Before Thatch had a chance to answer, the door swung open. An Asian woman stood in the doorway, holding out her hand.

Thirty-Six

"Hello, I'm Sunida. You must be Thatch," she said, her soft voice lilting with an accent.

Thatch put his hands together as if in prayer and bowed his head slightly. "*Sawadeekrab, khun* Sunida. Thank you for seeing us, and this is Tosca, a great admirer of Fuller Sanderson."

"Very pleased to meet you, Tosca," the woman said, smiling and shaking hands. "Please come in."

They followed Sunida as she led the way into the house. Tosca copied Thatch's gesture and raised her eyebrows at him in question.

"It's a *wai*," he whispered, "the way Thais greet each other." He kissed her ear on the last word.

They entered a living room. Tosca gasped at the contrast from the outside of the house. The room was decorated sumptuously with dazzling Thai silk wall hangings, colorful paintings of Thai dancers in exotic costumes, a teak sofa and three chairs with cushions covered in yellow and red striped Thai cotton. On the large bamboo mat were placed two knee-high, triangle-shaped standing bolsters, which offered back support in traditional Thai homes for those sitting on the floor.

A bronze Buddha head was on a corner pedestal, and incense burned in brass holders hung near the fireplace. A richly carved teak chest served as a coffee table, and a small hammered bronze gong occupied the east wall. At the rear of the room was a tall bookcase containing Sanderson's books, including those translated into foreign languages, Tosca noted.

No less surprising than the interior of the house was Sunida herself. A stunningly beautiful, petite woman with almond eyes, high cheekbones and waist-length ebony hair, she wore a crimson and gold sarong in the traditional Thai fashion. No telling how old she is, thought Tosca, searching the woman's face for wrinkles and seeing none. So typical of Asian women who never show their age until they're in their eighties and really irritating to us Westerners.

Thatch spoke a few words to Sunida in Thai, then turned to Tosca. "I told her how much we appreciated her willingness to talk to us. Don't worry, she speaks excellent English."

Sunida indicated they should all sit down. Thatch and Tosca took seats on the sofa, and Sunida sat on the other side of the coffee table. But she rose almost immediately.

"Oh, excuse me. I am forgetting my manners. I'll be right back with tea."

After she left the room Tosca turned to Thatch. "You speak Thai?"

"I told you, I spent time in Bangkok with a president or two on state visits," he said.

"I forgot, but you'd better tell me more later. I hate these enigmatic remarks you make and then forget to explain, and it's even worse when you smile like that Buddha head over there."

Sunida entered bearing a silver tray loaded with three lotus-shaped Celadon china cups, a matching teapot and a plate of flower-shaped cookies. She set the tray on the coffee table.

"*Kanom dok jok!*" exclaimed Thatch. "My favorite pastries."

Digging Up the Dead

Tosca kicked his shin, restraining herself from hissing, "Showoff!"

"I hope you like green tea," said Sunida, filling the seafoam colored tea cups. "If I'd known you were English, I would have made sure I had black tea for you."

Sorely tempted to correct Sunida by saying she was not English, Tosca said, "I am a great fan of tea of any color, although I can't see the point of white tea. It looks so anemic. Nothing like a robust cuppa you can practically stand a spoon up in."

Sunida bowed her head politely, and after more small talk she asked Thatch, "What do you wish to know? On the phone you said you knew I owned a tourmaline called the Chandelier, but I am sorry to tell you that it is not here at the moment."

"We know," he said. "We have it."

Tosca took the box from her purse and handed it to Sunida. Thatch went on to explain about Karma's party to celebrate Sanderson's anniversary, Sally's collapse and death, and how the tourmaline had fallen on the floor from her purse.

"I recognized it instantly," he said. "As a geologist I often follow the fate of extraordinary minerals and gemstones that are found, but the Chandelier disappeared from view very quickly. I wondered if it had been put on public display somewhere with its twin, the Candelabra, but it wasn't. You can imagine my surprise when I saw it the other evening at Karma's. Do you know her?" Thatch leaned forward, watching Sunida open the box, remove the gemstone and place it on the coffee table.

"I know all about the party," she said. "Someone I know was there, and he told me that Sally was rushed to Sheldon Hospital, where she died. It has upset me greatly." She paused, then said, "No, in answer to your question, I have never met Karma, but I know all about her, of course, as she's Norman's daughter and half-sister to my son."

Thirty-Seven

The bombshell Sunida dropped stunned Thatch and Tosca into silence. Tosca was the first to recover.

"Your son?

"Yes, Norman Sanderson and I had a little boy, Jeremy. He died of meningitis when he was three years old."

Sunida's face crumpled. She excused herself and left the room and returned a few moments later, dabbing at her eyes with a facial tissue. Tosca gave her a little more time to recover before asking, "Norman Sanderson was your child's father?"

"Yes. We never married, but we were mostly together until he died in the car crash with his wife, Destiny."

She told them she had met Norman when he traveled to Bangkok to research a book and was struggling to become as good a writer as his father. He attended a Thai dance performance at the Oriental Hotel and after the show asked to meet with any of the dancers who spoke English.

"I was one of the dancers," she said. "I could speak English quite well, because my father was a gardener at the British Embassy, and he taught me after he learned many words. Foreigners are entranced with our classical dance and the elaborately decorated costumes and headdresses we wear." She laughed. "Dancing, we all look very exotic and intriguing, but in reality we are just somewhat pretty girls, not the magnificent beauties that the silks, jewels and exaggerated makeup give us. I think Westerners find our dance techniques mesmerizing, especially the hand movements."

She paused to demonstrate, bringing her forefinger and thumb together and bending and curling her other fingers and wrist so far back they almost touched her arm.

"Norman wanted to know about the history of our dances, which tell ancient stories. The one I danced the night he watched us was a favorite with Thais, all about humans and gods, heroes, demons and other characters. Monkeys play a part, too. There are a series of more than sixty movements during a performance, and dancers start to train at the age of six or seven. I showed Norman the nine-inch fingernail caps we wear and my spired gold headdress. We ended up spending all our time together. When he left for America, he brought me with him."

Sunida told her tale in a quiet, assured voice, admitting she knew Norman was married and had a daughter.

"I didn't care. He was such a loving man. I knew he had room for more than one wife, and in Thailand minor wives, what you call mistresses, are the norm. Some of the wealthier men have four or five, and they often all live together. But Norman planned to divorce his wife and marry me."

"A harem," said Tosca. "But it's different here. What happened?"

"He had second thoughts about getting a divorce. He thought a scandal would ruin his career once he became a famous author, which never happened, of course. It didn't matter to me whether we were married or not. He set me up in this house, and he was here much of the time."

She stood up. "Let me show you his study, where he did his writing."

Sunida took her visitors through the kitchen and opened a screen door. Across the tiny courtyard was a studio. She invited them inside. Thatch and Tosca looked around at the bookshelves, file cabinets and a richly carved teak desk similar in style to the coffee table in Sunida's living room. On top of the desk were a laptop, a stapler and two framed photos. One showed Norman and Sunida standing in front of the Royal Palace in Bangkok, its richly ornate red and gold roof glinting in the sun. The second photo was of Sunida holding Jeremy as a toddler, his black hair and almond-shaped eyes similar to his mother's.

Off to the side of the desk were an electric typewriter, another laptop and a laser printer. Tosca thought back to the night of Karma's party and Fuller's staged desk with its carbon paper, pencil holder and pipe.

"Norman spent a lot of time in here," said Sunida. "I know he never produced a book, but it didn't matter to me as long as he was happy, which he was. Luckily, his father's earnings kept us all afloat, and after Norman died I was able to get a good job at the Ritz-Carlton Hotel, and I decided to stay."

She sat at the desk and slid her hands across the typewriter keys. "I didn't care whether Norman was a successful novelist or not. I loved him. Sadly, he never got out of his father's shadow and had very little confidence about taking on any kind of creative work. Maybe that's why he married an artist."

They were suddenly interrupted by a man asking, "Hello? May I come in?"

Oliver Swenson poked his large, blond head around the door. "Oh, I didn't realize you had company, Sunida."

"Come in, come in, dear."

Tosca's jaw dropped in surprise both at seeing the editor of Fuller Sanderson's books in Sunida's house and at how the Thai woman greeted him. Dear?

"Do you know Oliver? He was at Karma's party," said Sunida. "He's the person who told me about Sally's collapse."

"Oh yes, yes, of course," said Tosca. "Nice to see you again."

His demeanor was totally opposite to the surly man she'd talked to briefly at the fundraiser party. Instead, his large face split into a wide smile, and he emanated friendliness. He turned to Thatch.

"I don't think we were introduced that night."

In a jovial mood, far different to the stormy exit he'd made after Blair had taunted him at Karma's house, he offered his hand to Thatch, who shook it, nodding and smiling.

Sunida suggested they all go back to the house for more tea. They trooped into the living room, where Swenson settled himself clumsily on the floor, leaning his bulk against the tall Thai cushion and almost toppling it. When their hostess returned with a fourth cup and another teapot Tosca was struck again by the stark contrast between the two. Sunida's petite frame seemed all the more fragile compared to the obese editor, whose fat neck fell in upon itself by his awkward sitting position as he hunched over.

Tosca decided it was time to ask Sunida how she came to have the Chandelier in her possession.

"There's a very simple explanation, and Oliver knows the story." said Sunida. "Norman gave the Chandelier to me a few months after we arrived here in America. He'd heard the story of the Empress of China and her obsession with tourmaline. It appealed to his romantic nature, so when he read about the Chandelier being discovered locally, he went to the mine and bought it. "

"You must have been delighted," said Tosca. "I hear it is a rare piece."

"I was thrilled with Norman's gift. I know there's not another one like it. I have to confess there have been times lately, with money so tight, when I thought of selling it, but so far I've been able to survive without giving it up, thanks to Oliver."

Tosca remembered the silver locket that had fallen from Sally's purse.

"Since you know Sally, do you have any idea why she had a locket in her purse with the name of Abigail, Fuller Sanderson's wife, on it?"

"Yes, of course. Norman gave it to me after she died. It was another proof to Sally of my relationship with him."

Sunida went on to tell her visitors she had asked Sally if there was a possibility that Fuller deeded any royalties to Norman in his will, and if so, whether she'd be able to share in them. Fortunately, Norman had paid in full for the little house and put it in her name, so there was no possibility of being evicted, but the Ritz hotel was being sold, and she feared for her job.

"I was basically appealing to Sally's good nature when I asked her about the royalties," she said. "I'm sure she knew where they were to go because of her original contract with Sanderson. I needed to prove to her who I was, so I gave her the tourmaline and told her to take it to the Oceanview Mine. The owner would confirm that Norman bought it and had it delivered to me." She stroked the Chandelier and continued, "I was also willing to provide my son's DNA to prove Norman was the father."

Tosca glanced once more at the pair, still trying to come to grips with the paradox, the contradiction, of their body types. She was so tiny and willowy, and he was shapeless, paunchy and tall. Swenson's presence dwarfed the diminutive Thai woman.

"What about my book?" Sunida said. "With Sally passed away, can it still be published?"

"Your book?" said Tosca. What other surprises did Sunida have up her Thai silk sleeve?

"Yes, I have written a tell-all of my life with Norman Sanderson. Sally came up with the idea. I wasn't too happy about it, because Norman had letters from Fuller, his dad, showing he was critical of Tinky Blair. Sally said she'd provide a ghostwriter for me." Sunida glanced down at Swenson, smiled and said, "She introduced me to Oliver, here, and we've been working on the manuscript for months. Before we knew it, we had fallen in love."

The object of her affection appeared embarrassed and flicked a lock of his hair back, the same gesture Tosca had noted at the party. She'd use it in her article, she decided, as a way to describe the ghostwriter's habits. Her editor always wanted colorful details. He called it particularity.

Sunida moved over to Swenson and gracefully lowered herself onto the floor next to him. He put his arm around her, pulling her close

"We going to be married," he announced, a slight blush on his large face.

Thirty-Eight

This announcement was another bombshell for Tosca and Thatch. Both sprang to their feet to congratulate the couple, who got up to stand shyly before them.

Of the two, Sunida appeared the most embarrassed. Swenson's head was held high, a triumphant smile reaching from cheek to cheek. He was obviously thrilled to have won the hand of the beauty at his side.

"I never thought I'd fall in love," he said, "and here I am with the most incredible fiancée I could ever have imagined."

Tosca realized that Swenson was comfortable sharing his deepest emotion with the visitors and had no qualms about telling the world.

"When will you finish Sunida's memoir?" said Thatch after they took their seats again.

"I'd say in three more months or so. Sally was really excited about it, and we've been working very closely with her all along. Now that she's dead I don't think I'll have any problem finding another publisher. It's been our secret; no one else knows, and I think it'll be a bestseller because of the Fuller Sanderson connection."

Tosca asked Swenson if he planned to ask Graydon Blair to be his literary agent for the project. Swenson scowled in reply, shaking his head.

"No way. I hope to sever all ties with him very soon."

As soon as she and Thatch were in the truck, Tosca demanded to know how he'd tracked Sunida down.

"I still have a few connections around the various federal agencies, but this time I didn't have to ask any favors. Jeff Stanger gave us the address that was on the receipt, remember?"

"Of course. Why didn't I think of that? My powers of observation are being seriously compromised, living here in California. Everyone's too laid-back, and I have fallen into the same trap."

"Don't be so hard on yourself, Tosca. Relax. Enjoy the sun."

Tosca nudged the closed parasol at her feet. "It's the lack of rain, you know. It can addle one's brains." She fiddled with the strip of silk that kept the parasol closed. "Even so, you had to find out her phone number because you'd already talked to her before we went to her house. Google?"

"Yep. Real easy"

As they drove north he answered all her questions about his time in Bangkok. No, he hadn't been tempted by any of the delicate and beautiful Thai women, nor had he been tempted in Saigon, where the Vietnamese ladies were as graceful as butterflies.

Tosca finally lapsed into a skeptical silence for several miles, the Pacific Ocean on their left as they returned to Newport Beach. Every time she saw its sparkling blue expanse, Tosca liked to imagine the vast sea stretching silently up to the Arctic and west to Asia and Australia, then rushing noisily ashore.

"Not like you to be so quiet," said Thatch as they neared the bridge to Isabel Island.

"I'm starving. We never had lunch, and it's almost four o'clock."

"Sorry, sweetheart. How about we find a fast food drive-through?"

"Okay. I think a fish sandwich would fit the bill."

In Newport Beach they found a McDonald's, and while munching on their food, they continued to discuss meeting Sunida, trying to absorb the surprises she disclosed.

"It's amazing. There's the son she had with Norman Sanderson, the fact that she's writing a revealing memoir, her lovely Thai house, and most surprising of all, Oliver Swenson is her ghostwriter and fiancé. I can't believe how it all fits so perfectly together. The only questions are, why was Sally poisoned, and who did it? Did Karma find out about the tell-all? Would she have killed Sally to prevent its publication? Who else would have a reason to get rid of the poor woman? Ah, Graydon Blair, of course."

"Hey, you're at it again. Slow down, Tosca. Didn't mean to open the floodgates and get you going with throwing a bunch of questions at me all at once."

He steered the truck with his left hand and reached out with his right to envelop Tosca's hand in his large one.

"Don't go all dramatic on me," he said. "The cops are getting it all figured out. No need for you to get involved."

"Oh, don't worry. I am keeping my nose clean this time, but I dearly need some kind of dark, criminal activity for my next article. I'd better pay that nice Constable Parnell a visit. I know he needs my help."

They pulled up in front of Tosca's house. By now the sun was on its way to its inexorable evening rendezvous with the horizon before disappearing to the other side of the globe. She invited Thatch in, but he declined.

"I promised to take Christine out for an early dinner," he said. "I'm sure she's been sitting on the front steps for an hour already."

"Give my love to your daughter. Ask about her visit to the Alzheimer patients."

Thirty-Nine

At his kitchen table at home, Blair plucked at the strings of his Kinnor harp, cradling its small frame on his lap and appreciating the medieval shape and set of two bridges over which the strings were stretched. His callused fingertips and hands were a little too dry from the harsh scrubbing he'd given them after varnishing the front deck of his boat, but he knew that if he used oil or hand cream to soften the skin, it would deaden the tone of the chords he was testing.

After playing a few melodies he put the instrument down and picked up the chitarra battente. Strumming it gently, he heard a discordant note in its five double strings. Blair stopped playing and tried out the low D string to see if it was the culprit. Yes, time to replace it. It was a nuisance, because instead of the nylon strings commonly used on the instrument, he preferred to order custom gut from Denmark, and the waiting period was often as long as two weeks. This time he'd be wise to order a full set.

From the outside pocket of the harp's carrying case, he removed the tapered tuning key and unlocked the pin for the D string. Before he could unthread the offending string, his iPhone sounded.

"Karma, what is it?"

"You sound really testy, Graydon. I just wanted to let you know that Oliver has asked for a meeting with you and me. Sounds kind of serious. As far as I'm concerned, our arrangement with him shouldn't change now that you're going to find us a new publisher. We'll just go on as usual, right?"

Graydon took his time answering before he spoke.

"I can't think of a single reason why anything should be otherwise, but let's hear what he has to say. He's agreed with our plan all along except for that one argument the other day with Sally. I doubt Swenson will want to do anything different just because we're taking those manuscripts to a much bigger publisher. It'll be to his advantage. He knows we'll insist he be hired as the editor."

"Have you decided yet when the best time is to announce we've found them? My bills are piling up."

He hated hearing Karma's heavy breathing through the phone. "No. Don't do anything until I say so. That would ruin everything. When does he want to meet?"

"Tomorrow, if we can both make it. I sure can."

"Fine. Have him come to the boat at 10:00 a.m. We'll take a short trip down the coast. I have some brandy that'll soften him up."

Blair jabbed his finger at the phone's red circle to close the call. He finished removing the harp's D string and went online to place his order for the new set.

His thoughts returned to Oliver Swenson. Damn writers, always angling for more money or recognition, even one like Oliver, who knows very well that he must stay behind the scenes about books he has ghostwritten. The contract drawn up between him and the publisher was specific about non-disclosure. What could the man want? First Sally, now Swenson.

A knock at the door caused him to call out, "It's open."

He heard a voice say, "Oh, thank you. Terribly sorry to disturb you on such a wonderfully sunny morning. It's raining curtain rods in London at the moment."

That Brit!

"Mrs. Trevant, am I correct?"

He came forward and invited her in.

"Please do call me Tosca. We met at Karma's party. I was so interested to meet you. I know you were Fuller Sanderson's literary agent after your father died. How exciting to be privileged to carry on selling the works of such a legendary crime novelist. I'm writing an article about Karma's anniversary celebration and the fundraiser for a library. The evening ended in such sadness with Sally dying. A mystery in itself, don't you think, Mr. Blair?"

"A mystery? Oh, yes, the police were here. I suppose they interviewed everyone who was at the party, looking for whoever slipped Sally the poisonous sap they said she succumbed to."

"Oh, how alliterative you are. I'll use the phrase in my article, if it's all right with you?"

Blair's eyebrows drew together in a frown. "Do not attribute any quotes to me," he said.

Without expanding further and deciding he needed to be a little more hospitable to this gossipy woman who could be a threat, he asked if she'd like a cup of coffee. Shiny copper pots and skillets hung from a circular metal ceiling rack, and three glass-fronted cabinets held dishes and glasses. The bare white marble countertops and floor, meticulously clean, sparkled. Only the kitchen table showed signs of activity, and he watched Tosca immediately pounce upon it.

"Your Kinnor harp," she said, wonder sending her voice high as she regarded the instrument and reached out to touch it. "I hadn't seen one of these close up in years until I heard you play it at Karma's party. Where did you get it? What a beautiful instrument. How old is this one?"

At her enthusiastic barrage of questions, Blair felt disarmed. She sure knew her harps. He went to the Keurig coffee machine he kept on a side table and asked her preference.

"Espresso Roast or Perfetto? No, you look like a Mocha Swirl lady," he said, cocking his head and regarding her. "Or perhaps Tetley's British Blend Tea?" He held up the small K-cup.

"Thank you, yes, the tea will be fine. Oh, just a minute. You're brewing it in that thing?"

"Yes, of course."

"I'm sure it will taste wonderful. You Americans are so far ahead of us in many ways, but," she seemed to be searching for the right words, "don't you agree that tea needs to steep for a while, even when the leaves are reduced to dust and packed into those ugly teabags?"

"Sorry," Blair said, his tone breezy, ignoring her remark. "This is it. Did you take a good look at the Kinnor?"

He watched her run her fingers over the harp again, this time along one of its two horizontal curved arms, and explained he'd been tuning it up when he discovered the D string needed replacing. Blair complained at the length of time it took to reorder and asked if she played any instruments.

"No. I am a student of music, of opera most of all, and I've studied medieval instruments. I saw you playing this Kinnor at Karma's party, and late one evening we heard you on your boat—I assume it was you—playing a spinet. An ottovino, I assumed. You are multi-talented, Mr. Blair, or may I call you Graydon?" At his nod she continued, "You own quite an extraordinary instrument."

Blair jumped eagerly to his feet, clearly flattered. "Oh, this is just part of my collection. Let me show you some of the others. It's a small but highly significant group. I rarely let anyone see them, but I know you'll appreciate them."

He left the kitchen and returned carrying two stringed instruments under his arms and a third in his hand. He set them on the table along with a bow that he placed alongside the almond-shaped rebec.

"Do you know what they are?"

He was sure she didn't.

"Umm, let's see," Tosca said, peering at them closely. "They are basically all fiddles."

At his look of horror she laughed and said, "All right, but it's the truth. Anyway, I only know a few of them from seeing photos. This is a Welsh lyre, it's called a crwth," pronouncing the word as 'kruth' and smiling when Blair nodded in appreciation. "It's probably from the thirteenth century," continued Tosca, "and that one with the lovely bow looks like a Middle Eastern rebec, the kind Chaucer wrote about in his medieval work, *The Miller's Tale*. Such a pity it has a scratch. But this third one with a string missing has me stumped. A guitar, I'd guess, but what kind?"

"Well done, but I knew you wouldn't be able to name my Italian chitarra battente. Very few people can. It's a chordophone, belongs to the lute family. It's one of the rare smaller models. Medium and large sizes are much more common. Okay, I grant it's similar to a Spanish guitar, but I'm surprised that, with all the supposed knowledge of these musical instruments you've shown so far, you don't know this one."

He saw at once he'd hit a soft spot. Tosca launched into what she knew about the crwth and rebec, which was precious little, but she managed to make it sound comprehensive.

Blair let her ramble on, his mind distracted by the annoyance of having to order new strings for the Kinnor.

Besides, anything she said was of no interest, because he knew the background of his collection inside out, of course. Hadn't he studied their origin before figuring out where and how to obtain them?

Forty

After he served Tosca the tea, making sure to provide milk and sugar, and brought his coffee cup to the table, Blair sat down, but his mind drifted off again as Tosca kept talking. Her comments about musical instruments became a buzz to his ears, and his thoughts turned once more to what he thought of as the rescue of each instrument, a small smile hovering at the edges of his mouth.

He re-lived having to pull the rebec forcibly out of its owner's arms. The man wasn't supposed to be home, and Blair had expected a quick in-and-out mission with gloves the only necessary accessory. It was pure luck that the guy, a Jordanian diplomat, happened to be a collector of other items in addition to musical instruments. He also loved Arabian daggers, which were conveniently displayed on a nearby wall shelf. How easy it had been to grab one when the man refused to let go of the rebec.

Blair took the weapon away with him when he left, along with the musical instrument, and for a while he considered keeping the dagger instead of getting rid of it. He was intrigued by the fine hilt decorated with two silver rosettes and the gold adorning the handle. It was obviously valuable, but having the rebec was reward enough.

He looked at the crwth that sat on the table between him and Tosca and remembered its acquisition, too. Ah, yes, the young student from Cardiff, Wales. She had been in New York to perform as a member of a Welsh orchestra. As soon as he'd set eyes on it during the concert, he knew he had to have it. After the concert Blair went backstage, ostensibly to congratulate her on her skill with the ancient instrument.

There were too many people milling around to get close to her. He waited until all of them left, including the other musicians who told her to join them as soon as she'd finished packing up her crwth. Blair entered the room and said how much he admired the strangely shaped instrument with its two cutouts. He asked if she found it awkward to play because of having to wear a strap that went around her neck to hold up the bulky, square harp.

How enthused she had been to tell him that no, the strap was fine, it helped to support the instrument as long as it was placed correctly. Blair asked her if she minded demonstrating again the positioning. She obliged, slipped the strap around the back of her neck and held her hands in place as if playing. It was a matter of seconds for Blair to wind the strap, so conveniently in place, completely around her neck and pull it tight. She'd barely struggled.

He read in the newspaper a few days later, when the murder was reported, that this particular crwth went back to Roman times when Britain was occupied. The instrument had originally been discovered during an archaeological dig on land that belonged to the student's family. The crwth was immediately declared a national treasure and displayed in a Cardiff museum. The girl was given permission play the precious instrument only at international music events, Wales having realized its significance, and the museum as a tourism attraction.

"Graydon, hello!" Tosca said, realizing he was daydreaming.

"Sorry," he said, "I was distracted for a moment, thinking about the crwth. It's stunning, isn't it?"

She agreed it was most lovely and that all of them were the best of any odd, stringed instruments she'd ever seen.

"You said these are only part of your collection. What else do you have?"

"Only two others, a fourteenth century Psaltery, which you may know is a zitherized harp, and another kind of zither, a Chinese chyn."

"Way out of my field of knowledge," said Tosca. "I was wondering, when we heard you play the other night on your boat, if the sea air has any effect on them?"

"Not that I've noticed. I mostly keep them at home, though, and occasionally bring some of them on board to work on or play."

"May I ask you about this Baroque chitarra battente? It looks like a Spanish guitar, but I know that it didn't originate in Spain." She indicated the instrument. "What's its history?"

Blair was tempted to tell her that it had been the easiest to steal. His old-timer musician friends in New York had told him about an elderly Italian woman with a chitarra battente. She'd brought it with her when she immigrated to the States fifty years earlier, said it was a family heirloom. Blair had soon found out her name and paid her a midnight visit. Piece of cake.

"Its history?" he said to Tosca. "I really have no idea; I bought it at a second-hand store in New York. The owner didn't remember where or when he'd purchased it. Said it had been sitting in a corner for as long as he could remember."

He realized Tosca was standing up. "I'll have to come back and listen to you play each one in turn," she said.

Blair knew he'd better say nothing. No sense in encouraging her. He walked her to the door and thanked her for her visit, which he silently and fervently hoped she would not repeat.

After he ushered her out Tosca turned back halfway down the front path and said, "Oh, I must talk to you about Fuller Sanderson and his lost manuscripts. That's actually why I came to see you."

But Blair made no reply and was already closing the door.

She strolled slowly home, thinking about the man's passion for his musical instruments and his transparent obsession with owning them. Where had he found them all? The mini-sized spinet and the rebec were centuries old. She didn't know a lot about the crwth but knew one was displayed in the Cardiff museum as one of its most treasured artifacts. Was Blair's from the same era, or was it a copy?

Forty-One

Once settled at the dining table after breakfast, J.J. having left early again, Tosca booted up the laptop and Googled the square-shaped "crwth." She learned it originally came from Central Asia in the ninth century, eventually reaching Europe in the tenth and twelfth centuries. She was fascinated to read, too, that the instrument was a favorite of the lower classes and never made its way into a royal court. But then another document claimed the reverse. It didn't matter that much, but she did like to get her facts straight. Her newspaper editor was a stickler for citing reliable sources.

Tosca found several more articles relating to the archaic stringed instrument. One magazine story claimed that only four crwths had survived, one of which had been stolen from the Cardiff Museum seven years earlier. A photo of the last person to play it, a young university student from Wales, accompanied the article, as well as a photo showing her family weeping at her funeral. Despite extensive Interpol searches among private collectors, the crwth nor the strap that had strangled the musician had ever been found.

Was Blair's crwth the one from Wales? There was no strap with it, and she assumed the murderer would have disposed of it separately. The article ran a portion of the police report of the theft, noting that the museum director said there were no distinguishing marks with which to identify it, were it ever recovered.

The next instrument Tosca researched was the rebec. One batch of articles caught her eye. Several newspaper stories that ran consecutively for over a week in the *New York Ledger* said an extremely rare rebec had been stolen from a diplomat in New York eleven years earlier along with a medieval dagger. There were photos of similar daggers, detailed descriptions of the rare piece and interviews with Jordanian diplomats.

The thief, the police believed, had stabbed the man to death during the commission of the robbery, using an ancient Arabian dagger from the diplomat's own valuable group of six displayed on a wall near the man's body. The weapons were arranged in a star shape, and the photo showed one piece was missing. Like the rebec, Tosca realized as she read on, the dagger had never been recovered. The local police and the FBI had publicized the murder and theft widely, and the Jordanian Consulate had launched an extensive search, but neither the rebec nor the dagger was ever recovered and a murder suspect never identified nor apprehended.

Tosca peered closely at the photo of the instrument, then went upstairs to get her magnifying glass. Studying the photo of the rebec again, she saw a scratch on the side, similar to the one on Blair's instrument. Was he the thief? And the killer? Had Blair been in New York at the time? No wonder he was so secretive about showing off his instruments.

"Thatch," she said into her phone after dialing his number. "I wonder if you'd mind calling in a favor to that nice spy you know?"

"You mean Dan at the FBI? You're not off on one of your harebrained theories again, are you?"

"Of course not! What an idea. I merely wish to ascertain a fact."

"Tosca, whenever you use those kinds of words and that tone of voice, I know you're up to something wacky. If you're at home, I'll come over."

She assured him she was home and would put the kettle on.

"You mean plug it in," he corrected before hanging up.

"Yes, yes, plug it in," she muttered to herself, "but there's nothing like a kettle you can boil on a gas stove. I am positive water tastes better that way."

Fifteen minutes later she heard Thatch's steps on the stairs and went out to greet him, telling him that she'd just returned from a visit to Blair and tea was ready.

"And?" said Thatch.

"I will make yours iced."

"No, I mean, what's this theory?"

She indicated the sofa and brought over a cup of tea for herself and a glass of iced tea for her visitor. As he was about to take a drink, she said, "Graydon Blair is a murderer and a thief."

Thatch set the glass back down on the coffee table, shaking his head and suppressing a snort.

"Jumping to conclusions again. Tosca, you really have to stop hoping to find a corpse or unmask a murderer so you can go back to England. It sounds almost comical."

"This is no joke. I just knew there was something googly about that man when I met him at Karma's party. I could feel it in my bones.

"Googly."

"Yes, of course. A cricket term for when the bowler is a wrist spinner and turns the ball the opposite way than the batter expects. On top of that, didn't you notice how Blair twirled his cigar holder but never smoked all evening? "

"Lots of people are giving up smoking. Could be his way of quitting, like still clinging to his holder but not using it."

Asking for proof of her accusation against Blair as a thief, Thatch, seeming bemused, listened as Tosca related her conclusion by showing him the magazine article about the stolen rebec she'd printed out. She drew his attention to the scratch on the side and gave him the details of her time on Blair's boat and seeing his collection of musical instruments.

"So you see, *keresik,* all I need is for you to ask your spy chap if he can check out Blair's whereabouts on the date that the rebec was stolen."

She sat back on the sofa, satisfied she'd stated her case succinctly and had justified her plea for Thatch's help. All he had to do, she repeated, was find out where the literary agent had been eleven years ago. She'd already searched his web site, but there was little information aside from the fact that he was the agent of record for Fuller Sanderson's works. In fact, there was more space given to his father, Tinky, than to the son.

"And what will that prove?" said Thatch.

"That Blair was in New York and could have stabbed the owner of the rebec and stolen it. It's the same instrument. Bet he's got the dagger, too."

Forty-Two

After Thatch left Tosca's house he put in a call to the FBI's small satellite office in Anaheim that was an adjunct to the much larger Los Angeles bureau. He had kept in contact with two or three agents after retirement, and one in particular, Dan Delano, FBI Assistant Director in Charge, was a close friend.

"How about a few Stiegls?" said Thatch. "A six pack is cooling right now in my fridge."

"Hey, man, in exchange for what? Let me think. Finding the Holy Grail, locating Captain Kidd's treasure or discovering the lost city of Atlantis. Wait a minute, you're looking for Montezuma's gold. You still on that geology kick?"

Thatch laughed. "It's not a kick, Dan, you know I'm a serious hobbyist. Just got back from a rained-out trip to Idaho. No, come on over, and I'll fill you in."

He waited until Delano arrived before putting out tortilla chips, salsa and two beers. The FBI agent was still dressed in his office clothes: a dark suit, white shirt and striped tie. He followed Thatch outside to the patio that overlooked the Newport Beach Upper Back Bay and sank into one of the two wooden-slatted Adirondack chairs, sighing loudly.

"Rough day?" asked Thatch.

"Kind of intense. A lot on our plate at the moment. Aside from keeping track of potential local terrorist lone wolf types, of which we've ID'd three in Orange County, cyberspace hackers are proliferating, and then there're the usual number of pedophiles and bank robbers." Delano leaned forward. "What was in Idaho?"

"Fishing in Bear Lake."

"What did you catch, machinaws or cutthroat?"

"We jigged for trout, and I caught a sixteen-pound cutthroat, which I threw back in. I did catch a whitefish, though. Then we planned to go to the nearby rift volcano, but the rain was relentless, so I came back early."

"When I retire I might just settle up there along with a bunch of other FBI guys who already have. Seems to attract former law enforcers who are tired of the rat race down here."

Thatch bent down to open the cooler at his feet and handed his friend another beer.

"Dan, I need a favor. You can say no, of course, but I don't come to you with frivolous requests, you know that."

"No problem, buddy."

"As a matter of fact, it could mean just one phone call. I'm looking for a killer who murdered a Jordanian diplomat in New York eleven years ago and stole a rare rebec from his house."

"Uh, rebec?

"I know, I never knew what it was either. It's a kind of guitar. The murderer was never caught. Think you can help? I'm sure the FBI was on the case. The victim was a diplomat."

"Any other details?"

"Here's the diplomat's name and the name of the possible killer who calls himself Graydon Blair. We'd like to know if he was in New York at the time and anything else you can tell me about him. Oh, here's an article about the case that Tosca downloaded from the Internet."

"Ah, Tosca. Is she still cussing in Cornish?"

"All I'll say is that my vocabulary is improving. So, Dan, will you do it?"

"Sure, Thatch."

Forty-Three

Graydon Blair spoke into the phone, "Of course our meeting is still on, Oliver, although Karma won't be able to make it. An irate customer needs her to drive down to San Clemente immediately. No problem that Karma won't be here. You and I are the main players."

He heard Swenson mumble something about waiting until Karma was free.

"No, no, Oliver. Come down to the boat as planned. I'm polishing the handrails. Is this something aside from what the three of us are going to discuss? Okay, okay. Calm down. When will you be here? Right, see you in half an hour."

He kept on working till he reached the end of the stainless steel bow rail, then took the polish and rags into the cabin. In the small bathroom mirror he made sure his hair was in place. After putting the cleaning materials away and slipping the dirty rags into a bag to take home to launder, Blair remained in the cabin, sitting on the white leather bench seat at the small dining table where the Kinnor harp rested, two of its strings missing. Why are my strings snapping all at once? he wondered. From a large, thick envelope that bore several stamps from Denmark and two blue *Par Avion* stickers, he removed a plastic bag holding new strings. He took them out of the bag and placed them next to his musical instrument, pleased they were exactly as ordered.

Deciding to make the replacements after Swenson left, when he'd be able to focus on the tuning process more accurately, Blair lit a cigar and thought about the visitor he was expecting. Swenson had done a damned fine job, considering what an effort it required. He and Sally had been lucky he stayed on after Sanderson died. Now what could he want? The writer had almost fulfilled his side of the bargain just before Sally kicked the bucket, and his bank balance would explode in several months. Surely Swenson wasn't asking for more money?

Blair looked at his watch, saw it was ten o'clock and stubbed out his cigar. He went on deck to see the writer trudging toward the boat.

"Hello, Oliver," said Blair. "Come aboard."

Swenson was sweating as he mounted the small portable steps Blair had placed on the dock next to the boat for easier access. In the cabin Swenson could barely squeeze himself onto the bench seat opposite the agent and apologized for knocking the ashtray off the table.

"Not an issue," said Blair. "I'm glad to see you after that terrible tragedy at Karma's house the other night. So tell me. What's up? Are you concerned about your job at the publishing house? Karma and I are extremely satisfied with your work, and once we get the ball rolling you'll be a rich man."

"No," Swenson said, "I'm not worried about being fired. I know you are confident that the work I did is exactly what you asked for. In fact, that's why I am here. I wasn't sure who I should talk to about my plans. Do you know who is taking over at Hirsch House?"

"Haven't a clue. It's in chaos right now because Sally had run out of money, although I know you've been paid to date. My guess is it will simply go out of business. So no more Hirsch House. As I told you and Karma, we're going after the big international publishers."

He offered Swenson a drink, which was declined.

"Oliver," Blair continued, "what plans are you referring to? Are you joining another publisher? Your editing has been first class, and Sally had said that your other work is brilliant, more than Karma and I could hope for. We might even pay you a bonus."

Blair wondered if he was piling it on too thick. Like most of the ghostwriters he knew who were in the same line of business as Swenson, they weren't the type to suddenly produce an ego. Their contracts forbade them to go public. Everything they found out from tape recordings of a client and his family and colleagues was to be kept confidential, and when the book was finished, all materials that the client had supplied, such as tapes, photos, documents and letters, were returned. Have we misjudged Swenson?

To calm down the agitated writer, Blair hastened to describe the inquiries he'd been making to offer Sanderson's books to other publishers when he'd told them that the contracts he had with Hirsch House to represent Sanderson were now moot, given the bankruptcy situation.

"Here's the list of my contacts," Blair said, producing two pages of names. "I'm sure we'll get into a bidding war. This is really exciting news for you, Oliver, in light of what we are about to do. By the way, I need the flash drive. It wasn't in Sally's office."

"Yes, yes," Swenson stammered, "but that's the thing, you see. I'm not going to participate. I'm out. I never did like the idea to begin with."

He pulled a linen handkerchief from his trouser pocket and dabbed at the perspiration on his brow.

"What? You can't quit. There's no possibility of your quitting. The third book is only half finished."

Blair got up and went out to the deck, shaking his head.

Digging Up the Dead 179

Swenson followed him, saying, "Gray, my mind's made up. I'm getting married, and I am going to start with a clean slate. In fact, I am writing another book for my fiancée, a tell-all about the Sanderson dynasty. Your plan has bothered me ever since you came up with it two years ago. It's a sleazy way to honor Fuller. Honor! Ha! That's a laugh."

"You're wrong," said Blair. "The two and a half books you have ghostwritten are exactly the way he would have written them. In fact, they are even more dramatic than anything he's written. You've given the characters more depth and turned Johnny DiLeo into a much more complex and interesting guy. Come on, Oliver, tell me you're going to finish the third manuscript."

"I won't. I'm quitting."

"Now look, Karma and I have it all scheduled to be announced over the next two weeks. We're going to bring the media in and tell them we've found not only Sanderson's lost manuscript but a couple of others he left and that you've already edited them. So you see, we need you. No one will ever suspect you ghostwrote all three. What do you think of the titles? Very Sanderson, don't you think?"

Blair flicked the stub of his cigar into the bay as the two men stood in the stern of the boat. He continued, "We haven't quite come up with a story on how we found them. Karma joked we could say they were buried on the land Fuller left her, but then we decided to keep it a mystery for now. We'll string it out as long as we can. The media will eat it up. Two unpublished books we knew nothing about and the lost partial manuscript. This will go international, no doubt about it. Imagine the sales!" He turned to Swenson. "Come on, man, you're going to make a ton of money, too, plus what we've already given you. Let's go in the cabin and have a drink." He grabbed Swenson's arm, but he pulled away.

"You don't understand, Graydon. When I said I'm going to make a clean slate of it, that means I'm going public. My fiancée already knows what I did."

Blair stood still, as if turned to stone.

Swenson walked over to the rail and leaned against it, his thick arms dangling loosely, his head hanging down. He turned toward Blair.

"Sorry, I hate to disappoint you, but my mind's made up," he mumbled.

"All right, all right. Come on inside and have a drink. We need to talk this out some more."

"Nothing you say can change anything, but okay, I could use a brandy. I was so nervous about telling you."

The two went inside. Blair opened a door to one of the cabinets in the small galley kitchen where he kept several bottles of liquor. He came back to the table with two half-full glasses.

"Let's toast," he said, holding up his glass. "Skol!"

Swenson took a large gulp and set down the glass. "Wow, great stuff. What is it?"

"A Borderies 1914 Cognac Hermitage."

"Vintage, then. Must be pretty rare." Swenson took another large swallow, draining the glass.

"Yes, it is," said Blair. "I came across it in France three years ago. Notice the roast walnut and toffee aroma and taste? No, I guess not. The way you're wolfing it down, you're missing the entire experience of this marvelous old brandy."

"Sorry, Gray, guess I was unsure of your reaction when I told you my decision. You don't seem upset, for which I am grateful. Maybe we should all come clean, the four of us—well, three since Sally's dead and ..." His hand dropped the glass onto the table, his eyelids closed, and his head slumped sideways onto his shoulder.

Blair checked the man's pulse. The Ecstasy he'd added to the glass was a small amount but should have been enough to render Swenson unconscious.

Suddenly, the writer's head snapped up. "Geez, Gray, I must have dozed off," he said, slurring the words. His head fell sideways again.

Damn guy's like a sponge, Blair thought. He sprang into action, grabbed the strings he'd been using to repair the Kinnor harp and slipped them around Swenson's neck. Twisting as hard as he could, he watched them bite into Swenson's neck and disappear into the folds. An arm flapped in feeble protest as Blair continued to pull. He finally put his foot up onto the table edge to gain more traction, straining as hard as he could for several minutes. At last he let go and sank onto the floor, breathing hard.

"You know very well that I hate being called Gray," said Blair to the inert body. He went topside, started the engine, and pulled out to the open sea.

Forty-Four

One day later the news was all over the island. A man's body was found wrapped around one of the pilings under the pier. Two surfers had discovered it early the previous morning and called police. Tosca was irritated that she had already completed her morning walk and was back home when Arlene called her with the report.

"Tosca, did you see it?"

"See what, dear? Is there something up in the air or down on the beach I should be aware of? Really, Arlene, you are being somewhat vague."

"The body over at the pier. Don't tell me you don't know?"

Tosca sensed her neighbor smirking and enjoying one-upmanship.

"Are you having me on, Arlene? I know your nose was out of joint when I found someone's corpse that time and didn't tell you right away. Is this payback?"

"No, it's true. My friend called me. She watched the police arrive and take the body away."

"Well, dear, don't just sit there. Come over and tell me all the details. Is it still at the pier? Who found it? Who is it? Someone drowned?"

"I'll come over."

"Start at the beginning," said Tosca when she and Arlene were seated in the window nook at the small table. Arlene had brought her own mug of coffee, and Tosca had made herself a pot of tea.

"The body at the pier I told you about?" said Arlene. "It's Oliver Swenson! He's dead. Someone recognized him right away."

"Good heavens. How strange. Another one who was at Kama's party."

Before her neighbor could respond they heard sirens. Both rushed outside to see two police cruisers barrel down the street, screech around the corner and disappear.

"Where are they going?" said Tosca. "Come on, Arlene. As Sherlock would say, the game's afoot."

She urged her neighbor to hurry down the steps and into the street, following the route the cop cars had taken. They saw the cars parked outside Karma's cottage. The front door was open.

Tosca marched up to the officer standing in the doorway.

"What's happening? Did someone die in this house? We've had a death here already. You don't mean to tell me there's been another? Is this a crime scene?"

Parnell came out of the house, carrying a guitar sealed in a large plastic evidence bag. Seeing Tosca, he made a half-turn to go back inside.

"Inspector, I can sense your annoyance from here," she called. "Now what's happening? Karma is a friend of ours. Is she all right? I don't see any yellow tape to indicate a crime has been committed. Not another poisoning surely? Why do you have her guitar? May we know her fate?"

"Her fate, as you call it, Mrs. Trevant, is that she isn't here."

"Well, you can hardly blame me. I haven't seen her in over a week.'"

Parnell strode over to a cop car, placed the guitar in the trunk and got in the passenger seat. The officer at the house closed Karma's front door, and both cruisers sped off.

"How exciting!" said Arlene. "What do you make of it, Tosca?"

"Such drama. They're obviously looking for her. Probably have some more questions about Sally, although I am truly annoyed that the cops didn't ask Karma to come into the police station instead of frightening the ducks with all those sirens. Your customs often confuse me. John down the street has his cat on an antidepressant prescribed by the vet. How can anyone know the difference between a cat that's depressed and a cat that might be lovesick?"

They decided to drive over to Karma's garden center to see if Sam knew where she was. Arlene insisted that she drive. As they arrived they saw Kama getting into the back seat of a police car, which quickly drove away, the handyman watching from the shed.

Arlene and Tosca hurried over to him. "What's happening, Sam? Has Karma been arrested?"

"Nah, they just wanna question her, they said. She'll be back." He held out his forearm. Swollen to almost twice its size, it was bandaged from wrist to elbow. ""Look at this. She told me not to go weedin' in the milkweed patch. Doctor said I could've died. It's poison, that stuff. Killed that woman at Karma's party."

Sam shuffled off despite their pleas to talk some more. They looked at each other in consternation.

"This has really put me up a gum tree," said Tosca. "How am I going to pull my toe out of this hole?"

"What tree? What hole?"

"I'm talking about this complication. Don't you see? Now I've got to start solving Sally's case all over again. I was certain that Graydon Blair killed her somehow, probably by slipping her a mickey at the party, and I think I've figured out how he did it; but maybe it was Karma who poisoned her drink with that milkweed stuff."

"Oh, my," Arlene. "That's a hard one to swallow. Oops, I made a pun. Sorry. You know, she wanted to put one of those plants in my yard, and I told her I thought it was too ugly. But why would Karma want to kill Sally?"

"I happen to know that Fuller Sanderson's book sales are terrible. Maybe she wanted to get rid of Sally so she could get the publishing rights back from her and go to another publisher."

"That's pretty drastic. I can't believe Karma would murder anyone," said Arlene.

"You should read more books, dear. There are killers all around us."

"Is that an Edgar Allen Poe quote?" said Arlene.

"No, it's from a book written by a clinical psychologist who's a consultant at a prison."

The two left the garden center, drove back to Isabel Island and agreed to meet later on. Upstairs, and after fortifying herself with a good strong pot of Yorkshire Gold tea, Tosca decided to read the British newspapers on the Internet. It was a regular morning habit after she returned from her walk around the island. She liked to keep up with happenings at home, but this day she'd missed her reading session because she had a feeling the police would be on the island questioning residents, an event Tosca was determined not to miss. Instead, they left Karma's cottage without talking to her or to neighbors and party-goers.

Tosca logged on to her favorite online newspapers. What she read posted by *The Guardian* astounded her. Tosca switched over to the *Daily Telegraph's* web site. Same shocking news! She heard footsteps on the stairs and recognized them as her daughter's. Tosca rushed out to greet her.

Forty-Five

"I'm going home!"

"What?"

"Yes! The queen has decided to abdicate in favor of Wills."

At her daughter's blank look Tosca said, "Oh, come on, dear. Prince William. His dad and Camilla are being passed over as our next king and queen, and darling Wills will be crowned instead."

"Mother, calm down. That rumor has been around for months. Everyone knows it's not true. And take that maddening smile off your face, because it's never going to happen."

Tosca continued to smile broadly. "So you say, but the most revered newspaper in the UK says the rumor is probably true. Poetic justice, sort of, isn't it? This will be the second abdication of a monarch since Prince Edward gave up the throne to marry Mrs. Simpson. "

"Even if the rumor is true," said J.J., "how does it affect you and the lawsuit?"

"The palace can hardly engage in a sordid scandal when the world is going to be paying Her Majesty homage for her sixty years of public service. They won't want anything to tarnish her image. No, the lawsuit, even the threat of one against me and the editor, is dead."

She twirled around between the refrigerator and kitchen cabinets as J.J. continued to stand motionless in the doorway, racing helmet in one hand.

"Don't you see what this means?" said Tosca "I can carry a brolly again! I won't need that anymore."

She pointed to the parasol against the front doorframe.

"So you're happy to write the "Tiara Tittle-Tattle" column again? You were trying to get a promotion, remember?"

"Oh, everything's going to change for me at the newspaper. By the time I leave I'll have solved Sally's murder. The editor can hardly deny me a promotion to crime reporter."

J.J. harrumphed and went upstairs to her bedroom. In a few moments Tosca heard the bathroom door close and the sound of the shower running. J.J. opened the door, stuck her head around it and called down, "What about Thatch?"

Before she could answer, and her daughter was obviously not expecting her to, J.J. disappeared back into the bathroom. Ah, yes, Thatch. Well, I'll do a Scarlett O'Hara and deal with that situation tomorrow. Today I have a killer to catch.

She looked at the clock, decided that Thatch was either enjoying the afternoon sun on his patio or was out and about and called his phone.

"Yes," he said before she could speak. "I heard about the man found at the pier. I suppose you know it's Oliver Swenson?"

"I do, and I was thinking about Sunida. I'm sure she saw it on the news. How terrible for her. Should we pay her a visit?"

Thatch suggested they call first and ask if she'd like them to come over. An hour later he told Tosca that Sunida would welcome seeing them and added that he'd pick up a flower arrangement. He also advised Tosca that it was customary in Thailand to wear black, white or a combination of both, as it was in America, although he had no idea if Sunida followed her Thai funeral tradition or American.

Digging Up the Dead

Wearing a white blouse and black silk pants, Tosca joined Thatch in his truck, assuming that the box in the truck bed held a bouquet.

After Thatch parked at Sunida's house, he and Tosca went to the back of the truck. He opened the box and removed a silver bowl with several stemless white lotus flowers floating in water.

"It's the custom," he said when Tosca expressed surprise. "There's an Asian florist in Cerritos, and I made a quick trip over there. Beautiful, isn't it?"

"Lovely," Tosca agreed. "Certainly different and a charming change to the wreaths we give."

Sunida's front door and windows were draped with black ribbons. She answered their knock with a tear-drenched face.

"Thank you for coming," she said. "I am devastated, as you can see."

She led them into the living room, which had been stripped of the colorful cushions although the floor bolsters remained. The base of the Buddha head was swathed in a black cotton fabric and the exotic paintings were draped in ribbons like the outside windows.

Thatch presented the bowl of flowers, which Sunida placed in front of the Buddha.

"We're so sorry for your loss," said Tosca as the three of them sat. "Did Oliver have any relatives, and has a funeral been arranged?"

"He was closest to a niece, Terry Swenson, his brother's child. She's in college in Portland, Oregon, and her family lives in Roseville. When I called the Newport Beach police about when they planned to release dear Oliver's body, they said the investigation into his death is ongoing. I understood, of course. Then I called Terry. She had no idea who I was, as her uncle had only just proposed to me. He was going to visit them next week to tell them the news. I didn't plan to go with him at this stage."

A fresh paroxysm of weeping kept Sunida from talking further until she dried her eyes and went into the kitchen to prepare tea for her guests.

Thatch and Tosca sat silently until Sunida returned with the tray of cups and teapot, apologizing for having no pastries, and served the tea. Tosca again admired the Thai woman's delicate hands as she filled the cups, remembering how she was able to curve her fingers back so far, and pictured her dancing for her lover, perhaps in the study where Norman Sanderson wrote his doomed books.

"Are there any other relatives?" said Tosca.

"No," said Sunida. "Oliver had only one brother, and his parents are dead."

"Have they made funeral arrangements?" said Thatch.

"Yes, it's up to his brother in Roseville, Oliver's home. I don't think I'll go. I am mourning Oliver in my own way," Sunida said, attempting a smile.

Thatch got up, saying it was time to go. As Sunida accompanied them through the front yard, she drew their attention to a far corner of the yard that had been cleared of weeds and plants since their last visit.

"'I'm going to have a Thai spirit house over there," she said. "When I came to America I vowed to be as American as possible, and Norman supported me, but now I feel I'll get comfort from a spirit house." She shook hands then *wai'*d them both with a deep bow and went back inside.

"I know I can Google Thai spirit houses, but you may as well tell me now, what did Sunida mean?" said Tosca when they were driving back to Isabel Island.

Thatch explained that Thai spirit houses are miniature temples, very colorful and complete with steep tiled gold and red roofs. They are attached to a wooden or concrete pole and placed in a corner of the yard. They are said to contain the spirits of the residence. Their duty, he told Tosca, is to look after the family's well-being and assure blessings. Most spirit house owners light candles and place flowers on their small platforms when they wish for a special favor or outcome.

"It's a beautiful tradition," said Thatch. "When I was in Bangkok all the homes I saw had a spirit house in the yard."

"Thanks for the explanation," said Tosca. "What do you think will happen to Sunida?"

"Happen?" Thatch looked at Tosca quizzically. "What do you mean? She'll go on with her life, of course, like everyone else."

"She just seems so vulnerable, that's all," said Tosca, "losing Oliver Swenson so suddenly. They were so happy together. All right. I hate to change the subject but could you drive a little faster? There's a musical instrument I still need to research."

Forty-Six

Thatch took the 9 a.m. phone call from Delano while cataloguing the few rocks he'd brought back from his aborted trip to Idaho, which he had been forced to leave early due to the blizzard. Some of the rocks came from the Precambrian sedimentary formation in the panhandle near the Canadian border and had metamorphosed into slates. He put them aside to be set on a different shelf in his collection.

"Hi, Dan, any news?" said Thatch.

"More than I expected. I have to head down your way in an hour or so. Got a beer or two handy?"

"More than you expect," Thatch laughed and added, "just got a case in."

He tapped his cell phone off and checked the refrigerator. After counting the bottles of beer, he put six into a small cooler, took it out to the patio, placed it next to one of the Adirondack chairs and sat. The Southern California coast's infamous marine layer of low clouds, known as June Gloom, shaded the sun. The sullen clouds hung heavily over the coast, but he knew they'd burn off around 11:00 a.m. in time for Dan's arrival.

The two had been friends for three decades, meeting at first as professional law enforcement officers when their agencies cooperated on a case and soon becoming friends who shared similar tastes. One was the Stiegl beer they'd both enjoyed while on assignment in Austria and now made a point of drinking wherever it was available.

Thatch had taken early retirement from the U.S. Secret Service soon after his wife died of cancer. His son, a Newport Beach police rookie, visited often. Thatch's daughter, Christine, had been settled into a halfway house for functioning schizophrenics. She'd lived there for six years, since her twenty-third birthday. Like the other patients, Christine was unable to focus enough to hold a job but did her own grocery shopping and cooking. Her great pleasure was listening to music, and both her father and brother made sure she had plenty of CDs to play and iTunes gift cards for her iPod.

Agent Delano was in charge of the Orange County field office, reporting to the massive main FBI agency in Los Angeles. Thatch had sought his help in connection with a case he and Tosca had been involved in, and he appreciated the investigative facilities Dan had made available to him, particularly the forensics lab at Quantico, FBI headquarters in Alexandria, near Washington, D.C.

Thatch called Tosca's cell phone.

"Dan has some news for us. Want to come over?"

"On my way," she replied. At his house she went straight out to the patio and sat in a lawn chair.

"Hey, Dan," Thatch called out when he heard the doorbell ring and the door open. "We're out here. Just saw a light-footed clapper rail."

"Oh, no," said Delano, coming through the house and sitting next to his friend in the other Adirondack chair. "Don't go running those bizarre bird names by me again. You know I have no interest in ornithology. Hi, Tosca, good to see you again."

"But Dan," said Thatch, "this is a rare sighting. Okay, here, your first beer of the day," he said, handing him a Stiegl from the cooler. "Tosca?"

"Thanks, but I brought a flask of tea." She turned eagerly toward Dan. "What have you found out about the musical instruments and Graydon Blair? Where's the murder weapon? Was it the dagger? Have they caught the thief? Was Blair the killer?"

Dan popped the bottle cap and drank. "Let's take your questions one by one."

Thatch picked up the notepad at his side and looked expectantly at Delano.

"You sounded pretty upbeat about the results you found about the murdered Jordanian diplomat," he said.

"Yeah." Delano took several sheets of paper from the inside pocket of his suit jacket. "You'll see from these that we have files on him as well as his valuable collections of Middle Eastern daggers and rare musical instruments from that part of the world. There was one dagger missing from his wall collection, and amazingly it showed up four years later in France. Seems a hobo found it in a trash can, so our killer wasn't so smart after all. No fingerprints, but enough specks of the Jordanian's blood were in the hilt and the elaborate carving for testing. Since the New York police had a photo of the missing dagger from the Jordanian embassy, we were able to confirm it was the murder weapon, and DNA did the rest."

"How did it make its way to France?" said Tosca.

"We tried to trace its journey backwards but had no luck. The hobo probably sold it, and it eventually ended up with a pawnbroker in France who recognized it from a police flyer. He was obviously anxious to keep in with the police, and they contacted Interpol, who contacted us, and that was it."

"Okay, so we have the murder weapon but no connection to Graydon Blair. Anything on him and his rebec?"

"This particular rebec was almost as rare as the dagger but a lot easier to trace, because the musician usually needs to replace the strings at one time or another. The strings are custom made, and by contacting the few companies that sell them, we were able to put a list together."

"I knew it!" said Tosca. "There are always clues to be found in musical instruments. Piano wire has often been used as a garrote, and I read of a husband who recorded his violin solo in the highest C note and played it nonstop for two days, having tied his wife up in a chair. It drove her literally crazy. So, Dan, what can you tell us about Blair's rebec? I assume it belonged to the Jordanian?"

"Well, hold on now. His family has confirmed he was the owner of a rebec, but there's no proof it's the one your neighbor owns. Interpol agents are still investigating. We know it was stolen, probably by the killer, but there's no connection to Blair with either the dagger or the rebec at the moment.

"What about the deep scratch on the side?" said Tosca.

"Yes, there is that, but where's the proof someone didn't find it in an antique store or on eBay? One thing we are doing is checking out the people who ordered some strings. We can only hope Graydon Blair's name is on the list."

Tosca sat quietly, her eyes fixed on two figures in the marshes below, the man following a gliding hawk with binoculars, the woman holding a camera. But Thatch knew Tosca's mind was racing like a leopard after its prey, trying to come up with another angle to pursue that would give them an answer faster.

"Hey, sweetheart," he said, "let it go for now. No sense allowing impatience to get the better of us and coming to the wrong conclusion. How about we all go out for lunch?"

Forty-Seven

Arriving back at J.J.'s house after a meal at a seafood restaurant famed for its crab cakes, Tosca and Thatch went upstairs to find J.J. and Christine in the living room. They were talking animatedly and stopped when they saw Tosca.

"Mother, you will never guess what happened," said J.J. "Oh, hi, Thatch." She turned back to Tosca. "We went to six residence homes and talked to a lot of the staff and several patients with Alzheimer's, you know, for that music program I told you about that can help to bring back their memories. We let them listen with headphones and iPods, after we picked out songs we thought they'd heard as young people. Well, it worked!"

"You mean everyone began dancing and singing?"

"No, of course not. Well, a few of them were humming and smiling, so I know the program is a success. Christine," said J.J., turning to Thatch's daughter, "tell your dad what a great time we had."

Christine got up and hugged her father. "Hello Dad, we had a very interesting time. I only got impatient once! Just once!"

She went back to the sofa, smoothed her blouse and stared at the floor after her outburst, fiddling with the dark blonde hair she wore in long braids down her back, her fair complexion slightly flushed.

"That's great," said Thatch. "I'm real proud of you. But why were you impatient?"

"It took a long time for some of the people in the homes to understand why they were asked to wear earphones. It was so obvious."

"To you, Christine, it was obvious because you listen to your iPod all day, practically, but some of those elderly patients have never owned one, let alone listened to one."

Thatch had learned over the years, ever since his daughter had succumbed to schizophrenia six years earlier, to treat her as if she was as normal as anyone else. The disease had first struck when she was in her senior year in college. She had begun to hear voices and went through various phases of violent reactions to different colors, depending on the time of day. She finally dropped out and returned to her parents' house.

Thatch and his wife had scoured the country, seeking a cure. Finally accepting that schizophrenia in Christine's case could be controlled with medications but that she would never be restored to her former self, they found a private residential facility in the next town, San Clemente. The home housed five other semi-functioning patients who, like Christine, were able to grocery shop and cook their own meals but were unable to hold jobs because they couldn't focus long enough. There were medical staff who made sure they took their meds every morning and evening.

"Time for us to go, Christine," said Thatch. Bidding J.J. and Tosca goodbye, he and his daughter left.

Tosca poured herself a glass of mead and asked J.J. if she'd like a cup of tea, knowing full well her daughter never drank her mead, but J.J. said she hadn't finished telling her about the visit to the Alzheimer's patients.

"You're going to like this," she said. "A nurse at the third home we went to asked if it was at all possible to find some music played on a rebec, one of those rare instruments you told me that Graydon Blair has. She showed me a photo of a patient playing one he used to own. He asked if I had it, poor guy. When I told him I didn't, he asked me to find it for him. Isn't that amazing? I said I would do some research and asked if I could borrow the photo. Here, is this like Graydon's rebec?"

Tosca looked at the picture and noted the damage on the side of the instrument. It appeared to be identical to the rebec she'd seen at Blair's house, complete with the long scratch.

"We need to talk to this patient," she said.

"That won't help," said J.J. "The guy thinks he sold it to an Arab years ago."

"Aha. Then that proves Blair stole it," said Tosca.

"How do you figure that? Maybe that Arab sold it to another Arab. You don't have any evidence that Blair stole it."

"All right, I'll concede that, but this is definitely the same instrument. I doubt he'll tell me where and how he obtained it. It's easy to make up stories that can't be checked."

Forty-Eight

Dark hair blowing in the early morning ocean breeze, Tosca strode around Isabel Island's seafront at a quick pace. The marine layer was in full force at 6:00 a.m., but she welcomed its coolness for her daily walk. Several times she had hoped the clouds promised rain, but she'd come to accept that they dissipated by midmorning, and the sun and blue sky became picture postcard perfect. Darn. Was she never again going to feel the soft, sporadic cloudbursts that often marked the afternoon hours of her homeland?

As Tosca passed the house she always admired, with its Imperial concert grand piano viewable through the full-glass window, she wished she could hear its massive soundboard, but she'd never seen anyone seated there.

Approaching the Isabel Island ferry that carried three cars and dozens of passengers to the Peninsula and back, she remembered meeting Detective Parnell for the first time. The dock was close to the place where the Island's first-ever murder had occurred several months earlier. It became the case that started Tosca on her quest to become a crime reporter.

She pulled her attention back to the various pieces she'd gathered together in her current investigation, including the book manuscripts on the flash drive, the lab report of the sap poisoning that killed Sally and the unanswered questions she had about Graydon Blair.

Several imaginary crime scenarios flashed through her mind: Oliver Swenson informing Blair he was going to blow the whistle on Fuller Sanderson's fake manuscripts and Blair batting him over the head with the crwth. Or Blair gloating over his rare instruments and wiping blood from the rebec. How about Karma kneeling next to Sally after putting poison in her White Russian? Maybe the four neighbors had conspired to gather the sap from their giant milkweed plants and give it to their landscape gardener.

That last idea was pretty wacky, even for me, she reflected. What really happened? Why was Sally murdered? Obviously, to keep her quiet about something, but what? Oh, of course. The tell-all that Sunida was writing. As for Swenson's death, was he killed, too, to stop his Thai fiancée's book that could blemish Norman Sanderson's name? Yet, who would care? He was a failed novelist. However, Karma would care after announcing her fundraiser for Fuller's library. Wouldn't do to have his granddaughter accused of murder. If she was the killer, forget any fundraising.

So what or who was left?

"Chief Parnell? Ah, yes, it's Tosca Trevant. Pardon? Yes, of course I am still here in the United States. I'd hardly call you all the way from London. Kind of you to ask, though. I wonder if I might come over to the station later this morning and talk to you for a few minutes. Oh, yes, it's very important. In fact, extremely important. Good. See you in twenty."

Pleased that she felt she was becoming acclimated by using American phrases, she tried it out on her daughter who was curled up in an armchair nearby watching the news on television.

"See you in twenty," Tosca repeated. "Do I sound like a native, J.J?"

"No, you've got the rhythm all wrong, and the way you pronounce the T's gives you away. Besides, why would you want to do that? You've got people already mixed up when you speak in Cornish."

"Oh, all right. I just thought it would be rather respectful if I spoke like an American. When in Rome, you know the saying."

"Fat chance, Mother. You'll never make the grade, and I wouldn't want you to try. I love you just the way you are, although you might cut back on the mention of piskies because people have no idea they are Cornish pixies, and do stop forcing that mead you brew on the neighbors. No offense, of course."

"I know you don't like mead, J.J., but you mustn't discount the piskies. Dear little souls. I wish I had a couple in the garden. We did in St. Ives, you know."

"No, we didn't. I do wish you would stop this fanciful talk. You'll be spouting off about aliens soon."

Tosca picked up her car keys and sunglasses. "I am off to beard the lion."

On her way to the door she stooped down by the fridge, picked up a jug of mead and ran down the steps to her car.

At the Newport Beach police station, Tosca told the cop manning the counter in the lobby that she had an appointment with Parnell. The homicide detective came out with a scowl on his face. He waited for her to speak. Tosca put the jug of mead on the counter and pushed it toward him. He pushed it back to her. The cop behind the counter watched as they did it twice more before reaching for the jug himself and setting it on the floor.

"Whichever one of you wants this, it will be right here," the cop said. A phone rang, and he went to answer it.

"What did you want to tell me, Mrs. Trevant?" said Parnell.

"I know how busy you are, but can we sit down, Inspector? It's rather private."

He led her into a small room furnished with a metal table and two chairs. He indicated she should sit and took the chair facing her, a small notebook and pen in front of him. Again, eyebrows raised in query, he waited for her to speak.

"I'll get straight to the point," she said. "Oh, don't look like that, I really will. This is information I think you need about our two murders, Sally's and Swenson's."

Parnell spread his hands and sighed. "They are not *our* murders, but please, go ahead."

Tosca told him about the milkweed sap that was poisonous and the several clients who were growing it in their yards, and she concluded by declaring that anyone at Karma's party could have slipped it into Sally's drink.

"So now you have more than Karma as a person of interest," she said.

Before Parnell could respond, she continued, "Now as to Swenson's death, I have a theory about that, too. I understand that his body was found caught in the pilings under the pier. He had been strangled with something, my sources tell me. May I see the actual murder weapon?"

"Sources?"

"Yes, you know, those human beings who tell reporters all sorts of secrets. Sorry, but I cannot reveal their names." She sat demurely, hands folded in her lap. "I just need to see what he was strangled with. A guitar string, I am told, and you are questioning Karma Sanderson because she plays a guitar and knew the deceased, Sally, I mean. Thousands of people play a guitar. I suppose you have found a motive for Karma to kill Mr. Swenson?"

"We know the woman is broke," said Parnell. "Her business is about to fold, and she has two mortgages on her house that are in default. We believe she was counting on some fake books that Oliver Swenson wrote to resurrect Fuller Sanderson's sales and bring in a lot of money. We've already interviewed the writer's fiancée, a Thai lady in Laguna Beach. Not only were the two of them planning to write a book about her being Norman Sanderson's mistress with a child, Swenson was also going to reveal that he ghosted Fuller Sanderson's last book, and the supposedly lost manuscript didn't exist. Swenson's public confession would have ruined any future book sales."

"I am very pleased you have been so successful, Mr. Parnell. Has Karma been charged?"

"Not yet, but we're close."

"With the case so well wrapped up, would you have any objection to my seeing the murder weapon, the guitar string that strangled Oliver Swenson, the poor chap?"

Tosca watched Parnell consider her request. He seemed puffed up with satisfaction and took on an aura of magnanimity.

"Wait here," he said, getting up and leaving the room. Parnell returned three minutes later with a cop holding a plastic evidence bag, which he placed on the table in front of her. Tosca leaned forward, peering intently at the thin wiry strings curled in a circle inside.

"Could you turn the bag over, please?"

"Sure," said Parnell. "Looks the same from both sides, though." He picked up the bag, flipped it and placed it back down on the table. Before he could stop her Tosca ran her fingers over the outside of the bag. Parnell snatched the bag away.

"Mrs. Trevant! You are not permitted to touch evidence. This is a murder case, in case you've forgotten."

"Yes, it is indeed." She got up and turned to the door. "I appreciate your cooperation. I can find my own way out. A very good day to both of you."

"What the hell was that all about?" she heard Parnell exclaim as she walked to the reception area. "And I don't like the gleam in her eye when she touched the bag. Maybe it was a mistake to show it to her. I think she's done it to me again with that air of innocence. Damn!"

As Tosca reached the front door the cop at the reception counter called out. "Oh, ma'am, you've forgotten this jug."

"Give it to dear Inspector Parnell," she said, "He's going to need it."

Forty-Nine

By the time Tosca returned home from her walk the next day, showered, changed into shorts and a halter top and ate a quick breakfast, it was close to ten o'clock. She picked up the large, heavy file that contained the print-outs of the three manuscripts she'd found on the flash drive. Should she bring them with her? She decided to take only the title page of each book.

Tote bag in hand, Tosca arrived at Blair's A-frame house. Sandwiched between a two-story colonial on the left and a Spanish-style hacienda on the right, the Swiss chalet appeared to be squeezed from both sides, causing Tosca to wonder anew at the eclectic architectural styles crowding Isabel Island.

She knocked on the door. No answer. She shaded her eyes with her hands to look in one of the front windows, seeing only walls of shelves that held books and a few small sculptures, and minimalist modern furniture. No one. She strained her neck to look up at the topmost window in the steeply angled roof that came down almost to the ground-level outdoor balcony, half expecting someone to walk past the glass as if in a horror movie to see who was knocking. Determining that the entire structure was devoid of human life, she left the house and walked over to see if Blair's boat was tied up at his dock.

The Riviera bobbed gently at its moorings in the occasional swell that was rocking all the other boats.

Admiring again its sleek, elegant design, Tosca called out a "Hello."

"I'm up top," came the response from above.

Graydon Blair, at the wheel in the flybridge cockpit, peered down at her, a small smile on his face. "Tosca! What a nice surprise. Come on up, you haven't seen the view from here."

Tosca ascended the steps awkwardly, the tote bag on her arm banging against the handrail, and joined Blair in the cockpit. He patted the shiny white leather captain's chair next to the one on which he was sitting in front of the controls. Everywhere she looked the wood shone with wax and the chrome sparkled, and Blair himself was dressed sportily in a white polo shirt and green, red and white plaid Bermuda shorts that looked freshly ironed with a sharp crease down the middle. Who irons shorts? she mused. Obviously, the man who is meticulous enough to keep his boat in such a pristine condition he probably never sat down for fear of wrinkling his clothes.

"I'm just checking out a few gauges," he said, "and making sure I batten down the hatches, so to speak. There's a storm rapidly approaching from the Tasman Sea that promises to trigger some dicey swells over this side of the world in an hour or so."

"Oh, that's hard to believe," said Tosca, gazing at Santa Catalina Island visible twenty-five miles away. "The sea's as flat as a pancake. Of course, I realize we're in the bay, but the ocean from up here looks completely calm.

"You'd be surprised how quickly the weather can change when a storm hits," he said. "Surfers love the huge waves, but boaters know enough to stay home."

"I suppose you study the weather, being a boater?"

"As a matter of fact I am an official weather spotter and, as such, qualified to interpret weather conditions to help meteorologists make lifesaving warning decisions. I'm a trained member of the National Weather Service out of San Diego. They have a program that keeps a lookout for tsunamis, tornadoes, hurricanes and waterspouts."

"That sounds like a huge and important responsibility," said Tosca. "Do you wear a uniform? Have you won any medals?"

Blair snorted and ignored her question, saying, "Over there's my NOAA marine weather radio for communicating." He indicated a small side table where a square object was perfectly lined up to the table edge. Tosca reached out a hand to touch it and moved it slightly. Blair reached over and straightened it.

"NOAA?"

"National Oceanic and Atmospheric Administration."

"And what's that piece sticking out on the side?"

"A crank handle for charging in case the batteries go dead. It has a special alarm tone. That's how I know that the storm that began way off in New Zealand is rapidly approaching the California coast and is due to hit here in half an hour or so. It'll really kick up the waves."

"Oh, my goodness, I do hope it's going to rain, too. Even if the storm hits us, I'm sure we're safe enough here at your dock." She looked around the flybridge and its hardtop. "How beautifully open it is. No plastic side curtains to obstruct the view."

"I have them, but they only need attaching when it's raining. There are no current reports of that, just very strong winds, maybe of hurricane strength. Hey, it's getting close to lunch. How about an aperitif, a dry sherry? I have an unopened bottle of Domecq manzanillo in the galley."

"Splendid."

She moved aside to allow him to pass and go downstairs. He returned in a few minutes with a tray that held two half-filled cordial glasses set into molded spill-proof holders.

"And to what do I owe the pleasure of your company?" he said, handing her a glass. "Something we can toast to?"

"To Sally and Oliver," she said. "How odd that they have both passed on within a week of each other. Murdered, of course."

Blair raised his glass but said nothing.

Tosca took a sip of the Domecq, then reached into her tote bag to retrieve the three title pages of Sanderson's books.

"I'll get right to the point of my visit. As Fuller's literary agent, perhaps you can explain these?" She displayed each page in turn. "Ever seen them before?"

His mouth fell open, and he snatched them from her grasp. "Where did you get them?"

"On a flash drive we found on the floor at Karma's house the night of the party. Obviously, you recognize them. I was curious to read the document I found on the drive, thinking it could be the lost manuscript you were all looking for, but I soon realized there were three books, not one, and they had to be fakes. Who wrote them? Certainly not Sanderson." She watched him quickly recover his composure. "Graydon, I see you know exactly what they are. Do you know the author, or should I say, the ghostwriter?"

Blair was unable to hold her intense gaze. Eyes lowered, he said, "Why don't you believe Fuller wrote them?"

"There are a few things mentioned that didn't exist when he was alive. There's also a different kind of humor, the kind Sanderson never possessed or wrote. I should tell you that I studied the flash drive with the so-called manuscripts on it.

Own up, my friend. What's going on? This is superb sherry, by the way."

He watched her empty the glass. "Let me get you a refill."

Blair went down the ladder, taking the title pages with him. No matter, Tosca thought, I can print out more copies. I bet he's down there thinking up a story. Humph. Can't fool me. It's pretty easy to figure out that he, Sally and Karma were going to claim they'd found the lost manuscript and pretend to find two more later on. But Sally's sudden death put a spanner in the works, and they have to wait. In the meantime, I've caught them out.

A creaking sound came from the dock, and she leaned over to look down. Blair was unwinding the rope around one of the cleats that held the boat to the dock. The other cleat was empty. Perhaps the boat was tied up too tightly, she decided, and needed to be loosened a bit to allow for riding the storm that's coming in. I really should learn a little about boats now that I am living on an island that's surrounded by them. Our old fishing boats in St. Ives can't compare with these sleek models.

Blair came up the ladder, and she turned to take her replenished glass from his outstretched hand.

"Thank you," she said as he sat back down. "So please clear up this mystery for me. I'm going to get to the bottom of it, whether you tell me or not."

Fifty

Blair suddenly reached toward the controls on the console and switched on the ignition. The twin engines roared to life. He pushed the throttle forward. The boat shot straight ahead, leaving the dock behind in a tall spray of water and Tosca clinging to the armrest as the momentum forced her back against the bench. She managed to keep the glass of sherry upright, but some spilled onto her bare legs.

"Where are we going? Whale watching?" she said, unable to express her outrage at her kidnapping by the sheer audacity of it and saying the first thing that popped into her head.

"We're going for a little ride, Tosca. I'll answer all your questions once we truly get under way."

He adjusted the speed, and the Riviera settled down to a slower pace to conform to the boating limit of five knots while in the harbor.

"You haven't even asked me if I am free to accompany you. In fact, I was on my way to the dentist."

Blair turned his head to smirk at her. "I doubt you'd go there dressed like that; you are much too proper."

"Proper? Really?" A smile of delight lit up her face. "I'm glad to hear you say that, because J.J. thinks I am a bit of a strange duck, especially with my parasol."

He made no reply, and once clear of the harbor and into open water, he increased the speed, steering the boat into a wide arc before slouching back in his seat with both hands resting lightly on the wheel. Within minutes the weather radio sounded its alert. A metallic male voice broadcast a brief advisory about the fast-approaching storm.

Blair's gaze was fixed straight ahead, but he kept the boat circling a few times as the waves began to rise higher and higher. Frightened, Tosca decided to go down to the deck. No knowing what this madman is doing, but I'll feel safer down there, she thought, with the boat rocking the way it is. She got up from the captain's chair and was immediately overcome with dizziness. She clutched the stair rail to steady herself. Blair put the controls on autopilot and grabbed her arms, forcing her back into the chair.

"No, Tosca, you haven't seen my favorite place yet."

"I have no interest in seeing it."

"Ready for another drink? I see your glass is half empty again."

"No, thank you," she said, suddenly suspicious he might drug her. "The boat is rocking a bit too much for my comfort. Can you slow down?"

"It's not the boat, Tosca, it's the swells. The storm has come in from the Southern Hemisphere, as predicted, and pretty fast, looks like. See those clouds out there? They mean no surfing at the Wedge today due to the riptide. No one goes in the water, it's too risky. I'll know more when we get closer."

"Shouldn't we turn back?"

"We won't go much farther. I want you to see the Wedge at its most dramatic. "

"Graydon, while it is most kind of you to take me for a ride, I insist you take me back."

"Don't you want to hear about the manuscripts?"

Flustered at the abrupt change of subject, Tosca alternated between her panic at the turn of events, her anger at Blair's refusal to turn back and intense curiosity about the books she'd discovered on the flash drive.

"Ah, yes. The manuscripts. And Sally, of course. Let's focus on the publisher's murder first. I assume you were the one who poisoned her, and I believe I've figured out how. I noticed that you never use your cigar holder. I got a good look at it at Karma's party when you left it on the table. It's covered by a cap, so you certainly weren't using it to hold a cigar. Does the cap on it serve to keep something inside? A large dose of giant milkweed sap, perhaps, that you added to the White Russian you gave Sally?"

Blair twisted the wheel and made another sweeping turn, forcing Tosca to clutch the armrests with both hands as hard she could. The force of the action caused her feet to move back, kicking at her open-top tote bag under the seat. She gingerly released one hand from the armrest, reached down to steady the bag and make sure its contents were still inside. Her fingers touched her cell phone, her wallet, the keychain and the small cosmetic pouch holding a lipstick and tissues.

The boat had been bucking and rolling for several minutes, caught up in the waves that had increased alarmingly in height. Although they were still well in sight of land, the Riviera was the only boat on the water. On the beach she saw a small crowd of people gathered far enough away from the surf to watch the towering waves safely.

"I can tell you, Tosca, that you are right. I did poison Sally."

"Why?" For once she didn't pepper her listener with extra questions.

"Sally and I convinced Swenson to ghostwrite three books that we were going to claim were Sanderson's lost manuscripts. Not one, but three. Swenson has been working on them for almost two years. He'd already ghostwritten

Sanderson's own last book when the author was too ill to finish it."

"Yes, I read it and was a little taken aback by the slight change in style, but I knew Sanderson's health was failing, and I figured that as the reason for some of it being jumbled, and one or two threads in the plot left untied. Tell me more."

"Sally got cold feet about the three fakes we were going to claim were the lost books. She said it was too risky and, besides that, unprincipled. Stupid woman. Her business was floundering, and here we offered her a way out. That wasn't too bad, though, because I thought, all right, I'll break the contract and take the books to another publisher. I knew we'd get a big advance."

"I suppose Sally threatened to sue you," said Tosca.

"Oh, yes. She told us she was going to blow the whistle on the ghostwritten books. She also let slip she'd agreed to publish Swenson's tell-all. She had to be silenced, of course."

"What about the poison?"

Blair went on to explain how Karma told him about the toxicity of the giant milkweeds when he saw the blotches on her arms. When he commented on them out of sympathy, she blamed her own foolishness. She said her handyman had reminded her that the sap was poisonous, and she was a little anxious about the plants she'd added to her customers' yards. Then she'd nicked one of the stems by mistake.

"I jokingly asked her what the plants looked like," he said, "so I'd know enough to stay away from them. A plan was already forming in my mind. Karma took me to one of the front yards on the island where she'd planted them, so all I had to do was to go around looking in the yards and come back at night to cut the stems to fill up my cigar holder."

As she sipped more of the Domecq, finding its taste not so great after all and in fact somewhat sour, she listened to

Blair's tale with mounting horror as he set the boat straight and headed toward the coastline. Tosca breathed a sigh of relief that he was going back to the dock, but then her head began to spin again, and although she'd never been prone to seasickness before, she was feeling more and more groggy. Had he poisoned her sherry?

She let her hand holding the glass slide to her side, spilling the rest of the drink on the floor and dropping the glass. She hoped that Blair would think she was becoming unconscious.

I can hang on until we get back to the dock, she told herself, now that Blair has decided to give himself up by his confession to me. Through half-closed eyes she watched him standing up at the controls, gripping the wheel and barely able to keep his balance as the swells became higher and higher. He continued to head inland.

"What about Swenson, Graydon?" she managed to gasp. "Tell me about Oliver."

"The Tubby Ghost? He had to go, too. He got cold feet, just like Sally. He told us he was backing out and letting the cat out of the bag. That would ruin our plans, so I took him for a boat ride up the coast where it was clear that, sadly, he didn't know how to swim."

"But first you strangled him, didn't you?"

"Uh, yes, I did. But the cops can't pin it on me, because there's no proof. All they have is a guitar string."

"No, not quite, Graydon." Tosca spoke with an effort, the narcotic taking more effect. "You didn't use a guitar string. You strangled Swenson with the gut strings you were going to use as replacements on your Kinnor. I saw the difference when Parnell showed me the evidence bag. I know that gut has to be specially ordered from Europe. I'm sure Detective

Parnell will very easily trace it back to you when I tell him how mistaken he is."

Blair stared straight ahead, then turned and pointed to the right, toward the shore.

"Oh, look, Tosca, here we are almost at the Wedge. There's the peninsula. My God, look at the height of those giant waves! Must be thirty feet. Never seen them that big."

"Should you get this close to that jetty?" Her words came out with a hiss and she struggled to stay conscious. "Aren't you afraid of the rocks?"

"Too close? Oh, no. I know exactly how close I can get before turning away. I've done it a few times. No, Tosca, I thought you might like to see the Wedge close up and at its most furious."

He turned from the wheel, grabbed her arm and shoulder, lifted her bodily from the chair and shoved her off the flybridge and into the broiling water. "I don't have a body board to loan you, but it would get torn apart against the rocks anyway," he called as she sank below the waves. "Watch out for the riptide, it's an awesome, terrifying experience. It will kill you!"

He turned the boat around as if on a dime, despite lurching violently from side to side in the heavy seas, and sped away.

Fifty-One

The shock of the cold water brought Tosca's senses alive. She suddenly felt free of the effects of her drugged drink. Sputtering and spitting out seawater, she kicked her legs and rose to the surface. In an instant she was sucked back down again as the Wedge's infamous undertow tried to claim its latest victim. Her head hit the sandy, stony ocean floor, snapping her neck back.

The roar of the roiling surf as she was rolled over and over like a doll in a cement mixer told her she was in a deep underwater shore break where the land dropped steeply off, forming a strong backwash that dragged her down again and again. The noise was terrifying, as if a freight train was bearing down on her.

"Think, Tosca," she told herself. "Think. What did my father tell me when he was teaching me to swim in Cornwall? What was it he said when he made me swim into those terrible waves crashing against the rocks in St. Ives? Yes, yes, that's it. Swim parallel to the coast!"

The next time she came up from the riptide she twisted her body to the right, away from the rock jetty where the swells were the highest. She struck out as strongly as she could using the butterfly stroke, one of the most difficult to master but one of the most powerful and effective that her father had taught her. She focused on kicking her legs and using every bit of strength to swim parallel with the coastline instead of toward the beach. It was the natural instinct of every swimmer trying to escape the sea to head for shore, but her only way to beat the monstrous waves was to go against that instinct and fight her way through the troughs.

Trying to get into a rhythm, but having to crest some of the waves as they became smaller the farther north she swam away from the jetty, she managed to keep going. Every time her head broke free of the surface, her arm muscles burning with the effort of every stroke, she glanced toward the beach to ensure she kept it on her right.

She saw a small line of people watching the waves. She tried to signal them but the high waves blocked the view, and high winds were sending the sand swirling in every direction. Their faces were turned away, toward the jetty she had just escaped.

Tosca's sandals had been lost, and her shorts had been torn off by the riptide, but her halter top clung to her body. Deciding she had moved far enough away from danger, leaving the undertow behind, she realized she could now turn and swim toward the shore. The waves were still high, though, and she struggled to stay afloat.

Moments later Tosca believed she was close enough to the beach to feel firm sand beneath her feet. She let her feet touch the ocean floor. The water reached only up to her waist. Struggling, groggy and exhausted, her legs almost buckling beneath her, she managed to keep her balance long enough to step onto the beach.

Tosca lay down on the sand, gasping, trying to slow her breathing down to normal. She was grateful that her stretch bikini underwear had survived the trauma. In fact, she realized, anyone looking at her would figure she was wearing a two-piece swimsuit and had just finished a swim.

After a while she was able to stand and slowly looked around, believing she must have swum at least ten miles although, when she saw the Isabel Island pier jutting out on the Newport Beach Peninsula, it must have been only a mile or so. Satisfied and relieved she was now safe, she looked around. The beach was empty, the heavy, low dark clouds moving slowly.

"So I guess I have not landed in Fiji or Bali, then. Just almost back where I started."

She saw blood on her arms and legs where the skin had been scraped, but she determined it was mostly surface scratches from the gravel on the ocean floor. The worst damage was to her feet where the skin on the tops of her toes was badly lacerated. She sat back down again to rest some more and muttered. "Right, Mr. Blair. Be warned. I am coming for you."

When she felt strong enough to walk and seek help to get to a telephone or even a ride home, Tosca walked barefoot, shivering with cold and exhaustion, toward the nearest house. She was glad that the stormy weather was keeping people away from the beach. Despite her condition and the situation, she felt she looked an awful fright with bloody limbs and dripping wet hair plastered with sand.

Normally, beachgoers wore as little as possible and being shoeless and practically naked were common sights. The left side of her face was painful, and she touched the area carefully, deciding the long scratches on it, as if raked by fingernails, had been caused by the riptide's sharp undersea pebbles as she was dragged across the bottom.

She looked back across the beach to the Wedge, only several hundred yards away, where the huge waves were still pounding the shore. No surfers were brave enough to challenge its danger, and only a few people stood well back on the beach to observe for a few minutes before leaving.

Tosca realized she was on the Peninsula, a three-mile stretch of land shaped like a fat snake with the Wedge jetty jutting out like a striking tongue. The area was an eclectic mix of expensive homes and low-priced student and surfer rentals. The closer to the ocean, the pricier the mansion, despite being spaced close to its neighbors like those on Isabel Island.

At its west end the Peninsula fed into the mainland of Newport Beach and was surrounded by Newport Bay on one side and the Pacific Ocean on the other. This section of the Peninsula, Lido Isle, was crammed with restaurants, bookstores and galleries and was crowded year-round. Tosca and J.J. occasionally dined there at the Crab Shack, and Thatch took her to his favorite surfer bar near the beach. The other end of the Peninsula, where the Wedge was located, was almost palatial, judging by its homes.

Walking carefully down the side streets she wondered whether it was smart to knock on one of the magnificent wrought iron or carved wood doors to ask to use their phone considering the fact she must look like something the cat dragged in.

Instead, she turned and went back to the beach where the sole occupants, a group of young people, were huddled together, beach towels and blankets wrapped around their shoulders. The temperature was mild, but the sun was still blocked by the dark, low clouds.

"Excuse me, I'm so sorry to bother you, but I wondered if I might possibly borrow a cell phone to make a rather urgent call?"

The five teens, all holding beer cans, looked up. "You mean 911?" the girl in the blue bikini said.

"Um, no, not exactly."

"Wow! What happened to you?" The tallest of the boys stood up. "Were you in an accident?"

"Yes. No. Sort of. I got caught in the Wedge, back there," Tosca pointed to her left. The other teens got to their feet and crowded around, concern on their faces.

"Man, that's a dangerous place, we heard. It's a riptide. Nothing like that back in Omaha." He picked up a backpack, removed an iPhone and handed it to her.

Tosca thanked him and dialed J.J's number. No answer. *Re'm fay*. At the track, I suppose. She tried Arlene's number. The answering machine came on. Not home either. She knew Arlene's husband had a cell phone, but he was at work, and Arlene didn't use one.

Resigned, she called Thatch.

Fifty-Two

"Are you busy?" she said, trying to keep her voice light and cheerful.

"Filling up the truck at the gas station. What's happened? I can hear your voice quavering."

"I'm on the Peninsula, and don't have my car here. Would it be too much of an imposition for you to come and pick me up?"

"Sure, honey. Where exactly?"

"Right at the end of the road where it dead-ends at the Wedge."

"Be there as soon as I can. Don't go near the Wedge, though, the radio's been issuing warnings that the waves are terrible today. Might set a record."

Tosca handed the phone back to its owner, thanked the group again and walked the half-mile that took her back to where the jetty began. Heavy spray was hitting the warning sign like bullets, and huge waves continued to pound the rocks. She considered rinsing off the blood from her arms and legs but couldn't face entering the water again. She sat on the curb, dejected, and waited for the dressing-down she knew Thatch would give her.

Thatch drove up, parked, stuck his head out the window and waved. Tosca walked slowly over to the truck. The closer she got, the more his smile disappeared. He jumped out.

"You're soaking wet. Is that underwear? You're bleeding. How did you get here without your car?"

Thatch reached into the truck and brought out his jacket, placing it around Tosca's shoulders. He lifted her up in his arms, walked around to the passenger side, opened the door and set her on the seat.

"Right," he said, his forehead creased with worry. "What's the story this time?"

Tosca looked at him, bit her lip and began to cry, releasing the tension of the last several hours.

"Come here, honey." He pulled her into his arms. "Don't cry. Please don't cry. I never know what to do when a woman cries. Here, I'll take you home. You just snuggle down. I'll turn on the heat."

Thatch drove with extra care as if an invalid was in the next seat until Tosca said, "Come on, I won't break in half. I need to get home quickly and change. I have to talk to Detective Parnell, it's urgent."

She related the boat ride with Blair, his confession and his attempt to drown her at the Wedge.

Thatch said nothing, but his expression told her of his anger. He sped up, and they arrived on Isabel Island. Tosca brushed aside Thatch's offer to carry her up the spiral staircase, pointing out it narrowness, and took a shower as hot as she could bear. She didn't bother to blow dry her hair, figuring he'd already seen her in a sorrier state, and changed into a clean sweatshirt and grey knit workout pants. She half-hobbled downstairs.

"Honey, you should be in bed," Thatch said. "You've had a terrible experience. You must be exhausted."

"Aside from these bruises and a sore back, I feel a lot better after the shower. I might see a chiropractor tomorrow, but I'm anxious to talk to that Parnell as soon as possible." Tosca stretched out on the sofa and rested her head on a pillow.

"I'll see if he can come to the house." Thatch dialed and asked for the cop. "Not in? This is extremely urgent. Please try to contact him, and ask him to call me."

Two minutes later Thatch's phone rang.

"Detective," he said. "Can you come right over? We've got some urgent news about the Isabel Island murders. Okay, thanks."

"He'll be here in half an hour," Thatch told Tosca.

"Half an hour? Blair could have taken his boat down to Mexico by now."

"I'm going to see if the Riviera is docked, and then I'll check his house, but we need to wait for Parnell. Please, Tosca, stay here."

When Thatch returned he told Tosca that the boat was tied up, although the mooring lines looked as if they'd been hastily thrown around the cleats. The salon door was closed, and no one appeared at his knock. He walked past Blair's house and saw a car in the driveway.

"Looks like he's home," Thatch said. "Of course, he must think you drowned at the Wedge, so there's no reason for him not to come home. He's probably waiting to hear of a death at the Wedge on the news."

Before Tosca could reply Detective Parnell arrived, his face as dour as ever, and they all sat in the living room while Tosca related the day's events.

"He told me he'd poisoned Sally," she said in conclusion, "and taken Swenson out to sea and thrown him overboard, just as I said."

Parnell listened, his lips pressed together, then said, "Hmm. Pity you have no proof of all this talk."

"How about these cuts and bruises? And you could find the young surfers from Nebraska who were on the beach when I got out of the water. Come on, why would I make it all up?"

"Reporters have a reputation for exaggeration, especially the British tabloids." He got up to leave.

"Just a moment, constable, I have a recording of Blair's confession."

Parnell stopped in his tracks. "A recording? You mean you had your tape recorder on again, like in the previous murder case?"

"No, no, not my tape recorder. My cell phone."

"So let's hear it." The detective sat back down and looked at her expectantly, all traces of skepticism vanished.

"My phone's not here."

"Where is it?"

"On Blair's boat."

Thatch and Parnell looked at each other and then at Tosca in confusion.

"I had to leave my tote bag on his boat when he threw me overboard," she said. "It's under the seat on the flybridge."

She explained that when Blair suddenly started the boat engines and sped away from the dock on his way to the Wedge, the momentum caused her feet to knock against the bag under the seat. She pushed it farther back in case the contents spilled out. Later, when Blair began telling her about Sally and Swenson she had reached down into the bag as unobtrusively as possible, found the phone with her fingers and pressed the record icon.

"How could you do that without looking at the phone?" said Thatch.

"I know that the symbol for recording is on the left side at the top of the screen. I located it by feeling where the tiny on-off vibrating button is and then sliding my finger slightly over to the right and down. Really," she said, looking at both of them in turn, "it's not rocket science. So let's go to his boat and get my bag," she added brightly.

Parnell sat, pondered and looked at Thatch, who nodded and said, "Yep, need a search warrant. Otherwise, whatever's on her phone may not be admissible." He turned to Tosca. "It can be thrown out of court if the Constitutional rights of the accused are not honored."

"Oh, piffle. You two are such gormless wimps. Haven't I told you enough for a search warrant?"

"It appears so, but I need to make more inquiries," said the detective. "You've told me an interesting tale, and I'd like you to come over to the station tomorrow and make a statement."

Parnell thanked Tosca, shook hands with Thatch and left.

Tosca said she thought she'd better rest some more, and if Thatch would pick her up tomorrow to take her to the police station, she'd be very grateful.

"I can't stand the thought of dropping down into the Healey's low seat with this pain in my back."

Saying good night, Thatch made sure she was resting on the sofa, pillows behind her head, and tucked her up with the light red throw J.J. kept there.

"See you tomorrow," he said.

Fifty-Three

Tosca waited twenty minutes after the sound of his truck faded away before leaving the house. She went upstairs and changed into a black hooded jacket, black workout leggings and sneakers. Her dark hair, she knew, in the land of blondes was a decided advantage. She walked on tiptoe down the steps and along the sidewalk until she realized she must look ridiculous to anyone passing. She adjusted her stride to normal.

It was eleven-thirty, and many residents were sleeping. The only noise was coming from the bar across the small bridge that connected the Little Island to the larger Isabel Island. Tosca liked the idea of living on the completely residential and much smaller adjunct island, away from Isabel Island's busy, noisy commercial street. On nights like this, calm and windless, the sound of merriment carried over both islands.

Finding Blair's dock, Tosca approached cautiously and looked around. Good. No one taking a late night stroll, and no lights showing from his boat. She studied the steps up to the flybridge and shuddered when she remembered how suddenly and roughly Blair had grabbed her and pushed her overboard. She guessed Swenson had met his Maker the same way, imagining the heavy man hauling himself up the ladder with difficulty. Or perhaps Blair had killed him in the cabin downstairs. Yes, a far more likely scenario considering Swenson's weight. It would have been much easier for Blair to shove the writer's body over the deck rail and into the sea.

Digging Up the Dead

Tosca raised her eyes to the skies and sent up a silent thank you to her father for insisting she learn how to swim in rough seas when he knew how much she disliked it.

Looking around once more to make sure no one was in sight, she slipped aboard the boat. Grabbing the handrails, she mounted the ladder to the flybridge. At the captain's chair she'd occupied, she knelt down, reached under the seat and found her tote bag. She pulled it out and felt around inside. The phone was still there. She turned it on, careful to keep its bright screen shielded, and checked the battery. She'd been afraid the power would have run out, but all was well. I'd have looked a right pillock if Blair's confession wasn't recorded on the phone as I claimed, she thought. How Parnell would have crowed!

To Tosca's relief the phone had automatically switched over to the twelve-hour extra battery case she'd bought to supplement the built-in energy supply. After she returned the phone to her bag, she stuffed it back under the seat for Parnell to find when he had the search warrant. She looked around at the controls, the weather radio once more perfectly aligned on the side table. She grimaced at Blair's manic meticulousness and scrupulous attention to neatness.

At the sound of approaching footsteps, Tosca pressed herself against the seat of the captain's chair, hoping the person would keep going so she could stand up. Her knees were aching. Instead, she heard someone climb aboard. Oh, lord, not another boat ride. If whoever it was came up to the flybridge, she'd be discovered. She half-rose to peer over the side and saw patches of yellow reflected on the water. She guessed the person had entered the cabin and turned on the lights. As soon as she heard the first notes of the rebec being played she knew it was Blair. Although she didn't recognize the melody, it sounded like a medieval folk song.

Despite the situation, she sat back down on the floor, relaxed a little and, stretching out her legs as much as the small space would allow, settled down to enjoy the impromptu concert.

Tosca calculated that over an hour had gone by before Blair stopped playing and turned off the lights. He closed the cabin door and got off the boat. His receding footsteps gave her the opportunity to stand up and massage her cramped legs, reminding her of the time she had hidden in a closet at Buckingham Palace to await the arrival of a chamber maid to confide a few juicy details about a visiting sheik from Kuwait.

Tosca made sure no one was around when she climbed down the ladder from the flybridge. The cabin was dark, but as she passed it something twinkled inside as a nearby streetlight shone on it. Curious, she slowly slid the cabin door open and stepped toward the object on the coffee table. When she saw it was Blair's cigar holder, its silver band responsible for the point of light, she snatched it up and slipped it into her jacket pocket. What luck!

Walking home, Tosca felt the pain in her legs more strikingly than before and knew she'd have to take at least two aspirins. After closing the front door to her dark apartment and switching on the light, she wished J.J. was home. On second thought, she was glad her daughter was away. She probably would have kept too close an eye on Tosca and prevented her from leaving the house.

Fifty-Four

Just after 9:00 a.m. the next day, Tosca called the garden center and heard Karma's voice in response. She hung up without speaking, got gingerly into the little sports car she despised and drove the short distance to the center. Her arms and legs still ached from her ordeal fighting against the waves, but a sense of urgency drove her on. Just one more significant piece of the puzzle to set in place before she could go to the police.

After parking outside Karma's office, she looked around outside for the owner, then went inside, where she found her sitting at her desk in front of several untidy piles of papers.

"Hello, Karma, keeping up with things?"

"Oh, hello, Tosca. Yeah, so many bills to pay. What happened to your face?"

"Just a little accident at the beach," she said, waving a hand airily around and sitting on the chair opposite Karma. "Was the fundraiser a success for your Sanderson Library project?"

"Not as much as I'd hoped, but it all helps." Karma, her face wan, sighed and pushed the papers aside. "What can I do for you? A hanging basket? We have several on sale right now."

"As a matter of fact I was interested in your giant milkweed plants."

Karma stood up, brushing back her long hair. "Sorry, they've all been sold." Her tone was curt, leaving Tosca to wonder if it indicated a guilty conscience.

"I'm rather surprised they were sold rather than burned, considering the police told us all that it was the sap that killed Sally. Did you know it was poisonous?"

"Of course not! What a terrible accusation. The police believed me, and that's why I was released. Poor Sally. I've known her since I was seven years old, and Grandfather took me to her office. I didn't know the sap could be fatal."

"Yes, you did. You knew it could kill."

The voice came from the corner. Tosca swung around to where Sam was sitting on an upturned wooden tub. The bandage was still on his arm and dirtier than ever.

"Karma," he said, "you were the one that told me to be careful when I weeded there. I know I only got a rash, but you were darn definite about the sap being deadly. Look at your own arm. Remember you joked I shouldn't lick it? 'Course, no one in their right mind would go around doin' that. But you knew."

"Sam, those yellow rose bushes need mulching. Right now."

Karma's expression was ugly, but Tosca saw confusion there, too.

Sam got up stiffly and slowly from the tub and went out the door, muttering and shaking his head. Karma smiled brightly at Tosca and asked again if she wanted anything else, offering to show her some plants similar to the giant milkweeds.

"I have two pots of swallow-wort, if you like vines," she said.

"Karma, you're the gardening expert, so you must have known the sap's harmful properties. Did you tell anyone besides Sam about the sap? It would be perfectly understandable if you did. I know I'd warn as many people as possible about the potential danger. I mean, did you tell the people you sold the plants to? Was there someone you mentioned it to just in passing, perhaps?"

Karma appeared to have difficulty finding an answer. She propped her elbows on the desk, cupping her head on her hands, and closed her eyes. After several seconds she opened them and shrugged.

"Yes, I did know. I admit that, but I can't think of anyone I told except Sam."

"Not even at the party? You were wearing a blouse with very long sleeves that covered your fingertips, but when you were pouring my White Russian, your sleeve fell back, and I could see the rash on your hand. Did anyone remark on it?" Tosca paused, cocking her head to one side. "No, you couldn't have told anyone at the party because the killer had to have known days earlier to have brought the poison with her or him to add to Sally's cocktail."

Karma regarded Tosca balefully. "I have no idea what you're talking about. So Sally was poisoned with giant milkweed sap. A complete coincidence. Wait a minute." Her expression changed. "Yes, yes, I remember now. I was talking about it a couple of weeks ago and ..." Her words trailed off into silence. She shifted her eyes back and forth as if considering what she'd just said.

"You look as if something has just dawned on you," said Tosca. "What is it? When was this?"

"We had an argument at lunch a several days before my party. Sally had noticed the redness on my hand. It was much worse then, and she asked about it. I explained I'd cut the stem of a giant milkweed by mistake when I was trimming it to fit into a pot. I got the sap that oozed out all over my hand, and I told her it was some kind of poison that could be fatal."

"Were Oliver Swenson and Graydon Blair there, too?"

"Yes, they all sympathized with me."

"But what were you arguing about? Come on, Karma, don't clam up. What was the problem?"

"It was Oliver. Graydon had just told him he wasn't going to get as much of the royalties as he was promised for the books he'd ghostwritten. Oliver hit the ceiling. He was real angry and asked why not. Graydon said we were going to scrap the whole idea."

"Meaning there'd be no fake Sanderson books, no announcement that you'd found some unpublished works?"

"Right. It wasn't true, of course. Sally then jumped in and said two of the fake books were ready for the printer, plus she was going forward with the tell-all, and Oliver had completed the final draft. She didn't think it would harm my grandfather's reputation if it was revealed my dad had a mistress and a child. That's what readers still wanted, tabloid news, she said and reminded us all that the public's hunger for juicy, sexy stories hadn't changed since Madame Pompadour and King Louis XV."

Karma went on to tell Tosca that then Graydon had said that part of the scheme was cancelled, and he was going to take the newly discovered novels to another publisher. Sally was extremely upset. Blair told her to sue him, "which of course was impossible, because she had no money. So that's what we were all arguing about."

"I can imagine Sally's reaction. She was probably counting on the new books to get her out of her financial problems," said Tosca.

Both women sat lost in thought but got to their feet when they heard a police siren. As it got louder a Newport Beach squad car drove up and parked. Detective Parnell got out of the passenger seat and came into the garden center office.

"Karma Sanderson, we'd like you to come along to the police station with us, please." Although holding handcuffs, he approached her slowly and spoke politely.

"Are you arresting her?" said Tosca.

"Yes, ma'am."

"What's the charge?"

"Murder."

Fifty-Five

Tosca followed behind the police cruiser on the way to the station. Once there, she used the public telephone to call Thatch and tell him of the turn of events.

"Does Karma have an attorney?" he said.

"I asked her that when Parnell took her away, and she told me there was a lawyer friend of the family. She gave me his name, and I said I'd call him, which I am going to do now. It could be hours before she's allowed to get to a phone. He's Charles Carter. He was at her fundraiser party, the chap with the cane and the young wife with pink hair. Remember him?"

"No, but I'm glad Karma is getting representation. That's a hell of a charge. Sally's murder, I suppose?"

"Yes."

"Let me know if there's anything I can do."

"Thank you, *keresik*."

Tosca consulted a directory to find Charles Carter's office number. She called and explained the situation. Carter promised to come by the station within an hour.

After another half-hour had passed, Detective Parnell came out to the reception area and told Tosca she might as well go home. There was nothing she could do for Karma. Carver arrived as they were talking, and a cop escorted him back to the room where he could meet with his client.

The detective turned to return to his office when Tosca asked if she could have her tote bag back.

"Of course, Mrs. Trevant. I'll have it brought out to you right away. Good day to you."

Digging Up the Dead

"Um, would you mind waiting a moment, Sergeant Parnell? There's something I'd like you to hear."

"Hear?"

"It's on my cell phone, in my bag."

"Not another of your tape recordings? You said cell phone, not tape recorder."

Tosca made the smile she bestowed upon the puzzled man as sweet as possible.

"Yes, I do mean a recording. It's on my phone. Surely you'd like to listen to Graydon Blair confessing to both Sally's and Swenson's murders?"

"When and how did this happen?"

Clearly irritated and skeptical, Parnell's tone indicated he thought Tosca was pulling a fast one. He picked up the phone on his desk and spoke into it. Within minutes a policewoman came into the reception area, carrying the tote bag, and passed it to Parnell. He reached inside, felt around and brought out Tosca's phone, which he handed to her.

"All right, let's hear it."

She touched the phone to begin playback. As soon as Blair's voice was heard, Parnell asked her to turn it off and come back to the same room where he'd talked to her a few days earlier. He called a stenographer, who brought a tape recorder, and the three sat and listened to Blair boasting about how he found out about the giant milkweed sap from Karma and went around the island at night with a torch to find the plants. He said slashing the plants to collect the sap was "just like collecting syrup from a maple tree."

A small noise was heard in the background of the tape, and Parnell asked about it. Tosca stopped the recording.

"Blair took his cigar holder from his shirt pocket to show me the cap that covered it and how he scooped the poison into it," she said. "While he was explaining it to me, he dropped the holder, and that's the sound you hear. And, oh, here is that very same item. He'd left it in the cabin."

She brought the plastic bag containing Blair's cigar holder out of her pocket and gave it to Parnell, pointing out the cap that covered the opening for a cigar and the tape covering the other end.

"Hope he hasn't missed it," she said. "Perhaps you'd like to get it tested for giant milkweed sap and fingerprints? Yes, yes, I know mine will be on it, too, but I don't walk around with evidence bags in my purse, so I had to handle it until I got home and put it in this bag."

Tosca restarted the recording. They heard Blair telling her how he went around the island, gathering the giant silkweed sap into his cigar holder, then adding the poison to Sally's White Russian cocktail at the party while he was getting her a fresh drink. He had smiled as he told Tosca that he emptied the entire contents of his cigar holder into her glass, and it blended in perfectly with the cream and vodka. Then Parnell heard Blair's last words to Tosca and the thunderous sound of the waves at the Wedge. Barely heard above the pounding noise of the water was the gunning of the boat engine as he sped away, leaving her to drown.

"How come Blair didn't see you recording him?" said Parnell.

"He couldn't. The phone was still in my bag under my seat on the flybridge. When I reached down to steady the bag to make sure nothing had fallen out because Blair was going so fast, the one thing I touched was my phone. I realized I could turn on its recorder. I felt around, knowing where the icons were, and tapped the Voice Memos one. Luckily, it worked. So can you release Karma now? She didn't have anything to do with the murders."

"She's a witness, at least, to the argument and the fake books scheme, but yes, she can go home. I'll tell her lawyer and have her processed out. Here's your phone, Mrs. Trevant."

"Thank you, Chief Inspector. I'm glad to have been of help." She paused before adding almost under her breath, "Again."

He got up to usher her to the front door but Tosca wasn't finished. She continued to sit in the chair.

"There's something else you might like to know. You happen to have undeniable proof right under your nose here at the station that Blair killed Swenson."

Fifty-Six

Parnell let his head fall forward. "Don't tell me. What kind of evidence? Another tape recording, I suppose?"

Ignoring his sarcasm, Tosca said, "No, not this time. Something just as concrete, though. Something that is already in your evidence locker. It's the guitar string you said had been used to strangle Oliver Swenson. You do remember you claimed it was from Karma's guitar because one of the strings was missing, don't you?"

Parnell sat up straighter, pulled a file toward him and opened it. "Yes, of course. It was a logical conclusion."

"Chief, your evidence is not the kind of guitar string we usually think of but a custom-ordered catgut replacement for a musical instrument called a chitarra battente that Blair owns. I'm sure you can find the receipt for the strings he ordered from Denmark. When I touched the plastic evidence bag you showed me to prove the string came from Karma's guitar, I could feel right away I was touching double strings."

Parnell's expression changed from interested to skeptical.

"I guessed they were from Blair's harp," Tosca continued. "Guitars use single strings, but his chitarra battente uses pairs. Some use triples. Guitar strings are usually nylon or metal, but Blair uses custom-ordered catgut—not from cats, of course, that's just their common name. The strings are made from the small intestines of sheep or goats."

When Parnell's frowned, she added, "Don't worry, I researched the subject thoroughly in the *Encyclopedia Britannica*, the pinnacle of intellectual reference, don't you agree? The catgut is what you will find when you inspect your evidence more closely. So you see, you have nothing against Karma but plenty against Blair."

After Parnell dialed a number, muttered a few words and hung up, a policewoman came into the office and handed him the evidence bag containing the string from Swenson's throat. He opened it and removed the contents. He looked at it quizzically.

Tosca leaned forward. "You can see how easily the medical examiner could have mistaken the two strings for a single strand," she said. "It looks as if stretching and squeezing them so tightly around Swenson's neck caused them to bind to each other so that they looked like just one string. Catgut is a lot more pliable than nylon. It is extremely tough. That's why musicians who play harps, lutes, violins, guitars and cellos often prefer them."

"It may be more pliable, but I'm sure it would break if it was used to strangle someone."

"On the contrary, Inspector. Think of your own intestines and the terrible abuse they must take from what you send down there, especially if you don't chew properly."

The detective ignored her remarks and said nothing, appearing deep in thought and staring at the length of catgut on his desk.

"Where is Graydon Blair, by the way?" asked Tosca.

Parnell shook his head. "We'll pick him up soon enough, thank you. Why don't you go home?"

"The man could be on his boat to Mexico by now," said Tosca. "It's only an hour down the coast. Let me give you a hint, Constable, about his most likely intention. Blair would never leave without his collection of musical instruments. He'd risk anything to take them with him. They are his obsession. He's fanatical about them. I suggest you pop along to his house. Right now."

Parnell jumped to his feet, swearing, and ran out of the room. Tosca followed. She heard a commotion of car doors slamming and several vehicles racing out of the parking lot. She sat in thought for a moment before leaving the police station. Had she sent Parnell on a fool's errand? No, it made sense that Blair would return to pick up his musical instruments to bring to the boat before hightailing it to Mexico. He'd never, ever leave them behind.

Where exactly would the man go? Would he even flee? Blair didn't know that Tosca had survived the Wedge. But if he decided to take off, maybe he'd do the purloined letter trick in full sight on his boat among a group of other boats.

Thatch had told her about going fishing around some islands off Rosarito Beach on the Mexican Baja coast. The islands were uninhabited but a favorite spot for catching striped marlin and yellowfin tuna. The area was regularly surrounded on weekends by fishermen from nearby San Diego and Orange Counties. Surely, she realized, the Riviera would fit right in among the several other luxury sports fishing boats and barely warrant any attention.

Knowing Blair's arrogance, I'm sure he has presumed I drowned, she thought. Even now he might be listening to the radio or watching television for news about a woman's body being washed up on the beach yesterday, another victim of the Wedge.

She drove home, parked and jogged the six blocks to Blair's small chalet. Noting the police cars outside and knowing she'd be unwelcome, she headed for his dock on the off-chance he'd be there, or perhaps he'd left already. As far as she was concerned, Tosca decided, he must think I'm dead. He knows Karma was arrested from the media reports, but he must be aware she'd soon prove her innocence of any murder. Most likely she'd confess to having plotted with Swenson to write the fake Sanderson books, but that wasn't a criminal offense. The ghostwriter was dead, and thus the scheme was foiled. Karma would be free.

Tosca hurried along the last street that led to the water. With his back to her, Blair was on his dock, untying the remaining line from its cleat, the engine already growling.

"Well, well. It seems I'm just in time, Graydon." She stood behind him. "The police are at your house."

Fifty-Seven

Blair swung around, gaping at her. Before she could move he grabbed her around the waist and dumped her onto the deck of the Riviera, jumping aboard after her. He let go of the loose line, leaned over the rail to push the boat free of the dock and ran up the steps to the controls on the flybridge. The Riviera bucked like a horse when he increased the speed.

Tosca stood up, feeling fresh pain from the bruises she'd sustained, and mentally kicked herself for being so careless. Now what?

"Are we headed for the Wedge again, Graydon?" She shouted above the engine noise, looking up to the flybridge. "I don't believe there's a storm handy, is there?"

He glared down, increased the speed that sent sprays of water on both sides and raced toward the harbor opening.

Tosca quickly slid aside the cabin door and entered the salon. Should she find a knife with which to defend herself? Was there a way to sabotage the boat? *Re'm fay!* What a pickle she was in. She saw the ottavino battante on the table, its lid thrown back. On the bench seat were the Kinnor harp, the crwth, and the rebec. The two other instruments she saw she assumed were the Psaltery and the Chinese chyn. There was no sign of the theremin, and obviously he didn't value it. So Blair had already brought his entire collection of valuable musical instruments onto the boat.

She grabbed the rebec and the Kinnor, one in each hand, ran outside to the rear deck and held both instruments over the side of the boat.

"Graydon," she called up to Blair on the flybridge, "if you don't take me back right now, I am dropping your instruments into the sea!"

She dangled them farther over the side of the rail, secretly dreading she might drop one by mistake because her arms still felt like lead after her escape from the Wedge.

Blair turned from the controls at the sound of her voice, saw the danger his collection was in, swore and slammed the throttle back. The boat shuddered and made a half-turn as it responded to Blair's effort to slow it to a stop. He took a flying leap down the ladder, caught his foot on the last rung and sprawled on the deck beside her. He scrambled to his feet, his face drained of color.

The sudden slowing of the boat caused Tosca to grip the musical instruments tighter as the rail bit into her waist, bending her almost in half. Silly twit, she thought. Wouldn't it occur to him that his sudden stop could have caused me to drop the darned things?

The boat settled down in the calm waters of the bay, and she straightened up slightly but still held the rebec and the harp as far over the water as she could reach.

"Don't know what to do, do you?" she said, turning her head toward Blair and deliberately taunting him as she edged away to the far corner of the deck. "If you lay a finger on me, the Kinnor and rebec will be fish food. Well, not fish food, exactly, but very expensive hiding places for crabs and minnows."

The two were standing in silent confrontation, at an impasse, when a bright red Harbor Patrol boat edged alongside, a voice blaring through a megaphone for Blair to surrender. Tosca breathed a sigh of relief but continued to lean over the back deck with the musical instruments. Until a sheriff came aboard, she wasn't taking any chances, although she saw that Blair had gone back into his cabin.

The patrol boat came alongside, and one of its crew jumped onto the Riviera holding a rope. Detective Parnell and two sheriffs also boarded the Riviera. Blair emerged from the cabin to give himself up.

At this point Tosca felt permanently bent in half and wondered if her body would ever manage to straighten itself upright. Carefully and slowly, she stood away from the rail, still holding the instruments in stiff fingers. One of the sheriffs came over, took them from her and asked if she was all right.

"Just a kink or two, thank you."

Blair, white-faced, his shoulders slumped, was taken off his boat and onto the Harbor Patrol boat, where Detective Parnell snapped handcuffs on him. The Riviera was seized and taken back to Newport Beach to be processed for evidence. Tosca was helped as she climbed aboard the patrol boat and then was asked to come to Parnell's office to tell her story.

Four hours later she was home and calling Thatch. "Just had another trip on the Pacific Ocean, well, actually the bay," she said. "I must really like Blair's boat since I've been on it twice now. Oh, and he's been arrested for murder."

"I'm coming over. I don't trust these enigmatic statements of yours. Half an hour. All right?"

"Yes, *keresik*, please do. I'm a little tired, but I'd love to see you."

When Thatch arrived she'd already taken a hot shower and dressed in a sweat suit, her hair once again hanging limp and damp. She met him at the door and asked him to wait a few minutes while she finished drying her hair.

Digging Up the Dead

"Here's a nice piece of gossip that Arlene passed along. Sunida and Karma have met," said Tosca, entering the living room, "and they are liking each other. It's not a mother-daughter relationship but rather more of a close friend one. They sure have Norman in common and are exchanging reminiscences."

"Okay, but come and sit down. I want to hear all about this second voyage of yours."

Tosca curled up next to Thatch on the sofa and filled him in on her latest sea adventure. Alternately horrified and angry at her impulsiveness, he eventually calmed down.

"I'm going to make you some tea, and you are not getting up from that sofa until it's bedtime," he said.

Delighted with the attention, Tosca nevertheless called out instructions as to which tea to use, the Darjeeling, where to find it on the shelf, how to warm the teapot, where she kept the tea strainer, how much water to add to the electric kettle and on no account to allow the steam from the boiling kettle to last more than three seconds and how much milk to add to the bottom of the cup. She said the milk must be poured in first before pouring the brewed tea into it, because if milk was added afterward, it changed the chemistry of the tea. She told him how much sugar she preferred, two teaspoons, please, and added that it would take at least five minutes for the tea to brew before ready for consumption.

When she stopped talking Tosca realized that Thatch had found a teabag, an empty cup and the microwave. Ninety seconds later he handed her the hot tea. She thanked him without using a single Cornish cuss word.

Epilogue

Two weeks later J.J. came racing up the stairs and burst into the apartment. "Someone's parked in our garage! And the door can't close."

"Yes, love. I'm so glad your Porsche was off being repaired. Fitting my car in was a little difficult, but I did a good job, didn't I?" said Tosca. "The door will close when you move some of those boxes."

"That awful rusty old Jeep Wrangler down there is yours?"

"Yes, it is indeed, and don't call it old. It's six decades younger than your Dad's Austin-Healey."

"Mother, your car is pea green! Really bright pea green!"

"No need to shout, love, and of course it is. That's one reason I bought it."

She explained to an almost speechless J.J. that the Jeep's color could easily be seen by other drivers, and its lightweight doors made it easy to open and jump out quickly if the ground suddenly spread apart during an earthquake. Her choice of vehicle also gave her comfort in that it sat high, in case of flooding, which she'd also read about, except she'd neglected to remember that floods were mostly in the Midwest, and she also liked the rugged front grille because it provided a battering ram should she encounter a stray rhino. She said she intended to keep the car's soft top permanently rolled back.

"What if it rains?" said J.J. "The forecast said there's rain moving in. Look at the dark clouds!"

"Please. It never rains. Besides, I have my parasol."

J.J.'s expression told her how ridiculous she'd look driving around in an open vehicle, especially a pea green Jeep, holding up a parasol.

As if on cue, a few large droplets began to fall. Tosca whooped joyously. She donned her wellies and grabbed the parasol. She ran down the steps to the garage and jumped into the Jeep.

After driving around the block Tosca returned the vehicle to the garage. Upstairs, she took off the willies, left them outside the front door and shook the parasol, leaving it open to dry, although it was barely wet.

"Just wanted to see what it felt like, driving in the rain," she told her daughter. "Nothing like London, but it's a start."

Thatch knocked on the doorframe and looked into the living room, where Tosca and J.J. stood facing each other, arms akimbo.

"Hello, ladies. Am I interrupting a wrestling match? I've brought champagne to celebrate another murder solved—no, two murders solved—by our visiting sleuth."

Tosca and her daughter grinned at each other. J.J. took the bottle of champagne from Thatch and put it in the fridge. Without a word she and Tosca grabbed Thatch's arms and marched him down to the garage.

"It's hers, not mine," announced J.J.

After giving the Jeep a once-over and remarking how uncomfortable the seats looked, Thatch agreed that all the reasons Tosca told him for buying it were probably valid. He told her he was pleased she'd chosen a car with an automatic transmission, after the almost disastrous problems she'd had with the Healey, and the color would indeed be seen for miles as a warning to other drivers.

"That said, it's kinda strange you'd rather drive a big Jeep instead of that stunning vintage sports car."

"That's J.J.'s complaint, too. Nevertheless, you must both remember I am making a heroic effort to embrace America, and it is not easy, given how admittedly stubborn Cornish people can be. I am doing my small bit, because what could be more iconic and American than an aggressive, fearless, in-your-face battering ram Jeep Wrangler? Stop frowning, both of you. Let's go upstairs for a glass of mead."

Meet Author Jill Amadio

Jill Amadio hails from Cornwall, U.K., like the character in her crime series. Amadio has been a reporter in Spain, Colombia, Thailand and the U.S. She is a true crime author, has ghosted a thriller, writes a column for *MysteryPeople* ezine, and freelances for *My Cornwall* magazine.

Amadio is a member of Mystery Writers of America, Sisters in Crime and Crime Writers Association UK. She lives in Southern California.